RAVEN BOY

RAVEN BOY

BOOK 1

BY KATERYNA KEI

KEI Inc
2017

First published in 2013 by Kateryna Kei

ISBN: 9782954249216

Ordering Information:

Special discounts are available on quantity purchases. For details, please send an email to: contact@katerynakei.com

To Breandán, who taught me one of the most precious lessons in my life

To Tania, who was the first to like my story

FREE BONUS —

Raven Boy, A Treasure Hunting Quest

If you'd like some cool activities related to this book, you can download for free this print-ready activity ebook at http://www.ravenboy.com Enjoy! ;-)

Contents

Prologue

Long ago, the Earth was inhabited by happy, joyful, and never-dying people. They could easily change the shape of their bodies, turning from humans into animals or plants. If someone wanted to become an eagle, they could grow wings and fly; if someone wanted to change into a rose, they only had to ask Mother Earth for such a gift. And they could grow and blossom, giving joy to themselves and others.

But the Black God, who had sown so many evil seeds in the world, envied these good beings. So he divided each of them into man and woman. At that very moment, hate and vice appeared in nature; predators roared in the forests and plains; clouds of stinging insects rose into the air, craving blood.

And yet people learned how to find their sundered halves to become a whole being again. When the Black God divided the inhabitants of our world into men and women, each had an open spot on the chest. Through this spot the heart was seen; the heart that did not sleep even at night. When it met its other half, it would blaze with rainbow fire and longed to become a whole being again.

The king of darkness ordered the closure of the open heart-spot from childhood, so that people would not even hear the sound in their chest. Little by little, love went extinct in the world and everyone forgot the time when the never-dying people lived on the Earth...

From an ancient legend

The War Ships Return

"They are back! Konungr[*] Torgeir is back! They won!"

Turid abandoned her weaving and ran out of the longhouse.

Outside, attracted by the shouting, people hurried toward the sea. Everyone wanted to greet the konungr.

Two beautiful ships with striped yellow and red sails slowly, like gracious swans, glided on the sparkling water toward the land.

The crowd murmured excitedly, warmed by hope, curiosity, and impatience.

Just like the others, Turid spotted the ships from afar and frowned as a slight twist of worry tugged at her insides. It was just a presentiment, the usual woman's intuition—too small to talk about, yet perceptible enough to make her run faster.

From the first sight her suspicions were confirmed. Konungr Torgeir was not at the bow. His close friend Ari stood on his place, arm lifted to greet the crowd.

Her heart heavy with dark expectations, Turid made her way to the very edge of the pier.

Most of the people around her froze in apprehensive silence, every now and then interrupted by a whispered

---

[*] Konungr—king (Old Norse)

prayer or a sigh of relief when someone spotted their man alive among the crew.

Finally, the sails were lowered and the oarsmen maneuvered the ships to the wooden pier.

Ari spotted Turid and their eyes met. He said nothing; he didn't even move a single muscle of his face, but she understood it all as clearly, as if he had just shouted it: something bad had happened. The konungr would not return.

A couple of sailors jumped to the pier with ropes and started to tie the ship to it.

Without delay, Ari spoke.

"Peace and prosperity to you, my people," he started, and his strong low voice sounded official in the apprehensive silence around him. "We are happy to be finally home."

Several voices replied with a loud "Welcome!" while others just nodded silently, impatient to hear it all.

Ari was an excellent warrior, but a poor storyteller. Not that it had been a handicap for him—he sincerely believed a good punch to be more effective than long speech. So, feeling the impatience of the crowd, he stepped to the pier and went straight for it.

"We took their fortress. But our konungr is dead."

For the time of one breath everyone was silent, assimilating what they just heard, then shouts and sighs of pain, anger, and frustration erupted from the crowd. A woman started weeping loudly. Worry and foreboding filled all their hearts—the konungr was loved and respected by his people, and his death meant changes for everyone. It was all the more dangerous because they were in a war that was forced upon them by the Foreigners who had cruelly conquered some of their lands.

Then women pressed forward, all talking at the same time and pushing each other. They wanted to know what happened to their husbands, brothers and sons. But Turid was no longer aware of the mayhem around her. She felt as if she had been hit hard in the chest. She couldn't breathe anymore, and the world went dark. Her beloved husband was dead. And she didn't even see him go, she didn't even kiss him farewell! In her mind's eye she saw Torgeir as he laughed, as he galloped on his favorite horse, she saw him bringing her wild flowers at the dawn, playing with his sons, lying by her side on the grass and telling her about his love, his golden hair shining in the firelight… He was so alive in her mind that it was all the harder to realize that from now on this man was gone. Gone forever! Dead! From now on, she was alone. From now on, she was a widow. Never again will he mischievously wink at her in the middle of an important assembly, never again will he kiss her and lift her in his strong, tender arms, never again will he hug her in his sleep…

A piercing, painful emptiness swept over her, tearing every inch of her body. She would have collapsed, but a strong, caring hand seized her shoulder and stopped her. The warmth and firmness of this touch was somewhat consoling, and she slowly returned back to reality.

Her youngest son, Hrafn, stood by her side, his hand on her shoulder. Turid met his gaze and they remained motionless for a moment, silently sharing the pain and comforting each other. Somehow, the boy's presence and silent support made it easier to bear.

Then Turid's eldest son, Olaf, joined them as well. Tears shone in his darkened gray eyes. Yet none of them cried— not in front of everybody. Together, they made their way through the crowd and back to the longhouse.

As they passed, people bowed or muttered words of compassion. But the widow and her sons were beyond noticing. Her rank separated her from other women; Turid was denied the time to cry her pain out. As queen, she was in charge of everything when her husband wasn't there, and the return of the warriors meant additional work that needed to be done. On the dreadful walk from the docks to the village, she struggled to pull herself together, to push all the hurting thoughts to some far corner of her mind and to lock them there for a while.

Her sons held her hands. Her brave little men stoically fought off their own tears and pain. She had to be strong too. For them and for her people.

For the good memory of her beloved husband.

This fresh thought of Torgeir brought another huge wave of pain on her. Before it would swallow her completely, Turid screwed her eyes shut and took several deep breaths. Her mother had always told her that breathing was the best remedy, the fastest way to regain the self-control.

When she looked at her sons again, both regarded her with apprehension.

"Olaf, Hrafn, I am sorry. There is no time to mourn now. I must take care of the warriors and organize the feast…"

She wanted to say "in Torgeir's memory," but the words just wouldn't come out.

She couldn't decide what was better—to let the children go home or to keep them busy with something, but they solved it for her.

"Can we stay and help you?" asked Hrafn and Olaf nodded, looking hopeful.

A sudden surge of tenderness toward her twins brought tears to her eyes and she hugged both of them, unable to utter a word.

~~~
~~~

Staying busy was sufficient to keep painful thoughts and grief at bay. Too many things had to be done and thought through, and even people's condolences and words of compassion seemed somehow much easier to bear. Probably it was so because Turid just didn't have time to think. She was able to sit down only at the feast, but could not force herself to eat or drink, knowing that soon the details of her husband's death would be revealed. Turid wanted to know it all, and at the same time dreaded it.

But Olaf and Hrafn dreaded something else even more.

Two winters ago they saw the funeral of jarl[*] Yngve from the neighboring fjord. Yngve had a wife and two mistresses and by the tradition after his death they were asked whether one of them would like to join him. One of his mistresses said yes. At the end of the ceremony, she was burned in the ship, next to her dead lover.

Their father had no mistresses, only his wife, their mother. The boys feared that she would choose to die and thus they would lose both their parents at once. Olaf and Hrafn sat through the feast quiet and tense, studying their mother's face and behavior and trying to guess what was about to come.

When the time came, the storyteller stepped forward with his harp. His name was Orm. He was a warrior just as tall and muscled as the other Vikings, but his hair and beard were completely gray and his sun-browned face was even more lined.

He cleared his voice and began. "As all of you surely know, a month ago our brave Konungr Torgeir led three of our ships to war with the evil Foreigners.

---

[*] Jarl—earl (Old Norse). The word « jarl » meant a chieftain set to rule a territory in a king's stead.

"We have never sailed to their lands before, but knew the way from merchants and travelers.

"We traveled for seven days. The sky was clear and blue and the wind was fair, as if Gods were on our side, propelling us forward and helping us. Hope filled our hearts as we readied for the battle.

"But then a storm broke out…"

He took a deep breath. Hypnotized, the crowd did just the same, catching his every word.

"Dark, heavy clouds covered the sky very fast and came down so low, that the tops of our masts scratched them. We lowered our sails and masts as blasts of cold wind fell upon us. Waves towered over the ships, trying to swallow us completely. The planks shivered and moaned under our feet and cold salty water filled our ship faster than we were able to bucket it.

"Separated by the storm, each ship fought on her own against the sea gods. They played with us for quite a while, throwing the ships like pieces of straw. Then, all of a sudden, rocks appeared in front of us, emerging from the foaming, angry waves. More and more of them appeared, higher and higher they grew. They looked like terrible fanged monsters waiting for new prey. We all thought that the ship would break on them, for the sea gods carried us toward those rocks. But an excellent sailor as he always was, Torgeir spotted an opening between the rocky teeth. He must have felt there was a bay there. He skillfully rode a big wave and made it carry the ship into the bay.

"We stopped rowing and looked around. The sea was much calmer there, and tall, black rocks disappeared in the darkness far above us and seemed to form a huge cavern. At least we thought so, judging by the sound, for it was too dark to see well. As we were most likely on the enemy's territory, we didn't light torches and spent the night in the dark, just floating there, while the storm raged outside.

"The night was over, yet we were still unable to see. The morning light reached us at last, but instead of black darkness, we were now in the middle of a deep, white fog. White like milk, it was so dense, that one could not see his own feet. No one knew how long it lasted; we could only tell that it was still day when it started to dissipate. Then we saw that the cavern had a quite large opening at the top and was wide enough to contain two dozens of ships. It led to the dry land where beautiful trees and flowers grew. And we saw that six large enemy boats were floating there around us, ready to attack…"

His audience held their breath, eagerly catching his every word.

"We knew we were doomed, but none of us gave thought to surrendering. As for the enemy, they attacked, rushing toward us like wolves charging on a deer…

"It was a fierce fight. We were surrounded. Torgeir and a group of warriors were positioned alongside the boards, protecting the ship as best as they could. Others received the order to row. First, they fired arrows at us, wounding some and killing Bjarte and Calder, valiant men and good friends who remain in our memory while they feast in Valhalla.

"When the Foreigners were close enough, they threw boarding hooks, trying to get on our ship.

"We fought like never before. Torgeir was everywhere: cutting their ropes, covering for the oarsmen, shouting orders and throwing spears—a weapon that he mastered better than anyone alive. He wanted us out of the bay so badly, that he finally did something mad, brave and unexpected: together with Halvdan and Gudmund, he jumped on the enemy ship that was between us and the entrance to the bay. Taking advantage of the Foreigners' surprise, they killed several warriors at once and managed to shift their sail. The Foreigners didn't notice it right away, and these seconds saved our lives. Torgeir, Halvdan and Gudmund kept fighting as if it had been their only aim, while the shifted sail caught the wind coming from the bay entrance, and the ship moved out of our way.

"We were ready. Those who had been fighting instantly dropped their weapons and we pushed hard on our oars. Our sail was down, and the wind couldn't keep us from rushing forward. Those who were up front didn't have time to pull their oars out. They broke with a loud cracking against the stern of the enemy ship. But we managed to keep our ship straight, heading toward the opening in the rocks.

"Meanwhile, Halvdan and Gudmund were slain. They fought bravely, taking at least a dozen of Foreigners with them each. Torgeir was wounded but still fought. He shouted us to keep going. But Ari didn't want to leave his friend in the hands of the Foreigners. He tied a long rope to the mast, and as our ship passed by the foreign boat where Torgeir was still fighting, he jumped on it. In this one jump, he killed three people and caught Torgeir, bringing him back to our ship. We madly rowed under the hail of arrows, and Torgeir and Ari joined us.

"It must have been quick, but it seemed to us too long, the time before we reached the opening and passed through it toward the setting sun, reflected in the open sea. The Foreign boats were close behind, determined not to let us go. One by one, they appeared out of the opening, still firing arrows that hardly reached us, thanks to the wind.

"And finally the gods turned toward us—our two other ships were there, at the ready, hurrying into the battle.

"The Foreigners obviously did not expect it, for they

stopped firing arrows and seemed hesitant. But we didn't give them the time to think: at Torgeir's order our ships attacked, propelled by the fair wind in their sails. We hoisted the sail and adjusted the number of oars on each side before joining them. The Foreigners still outnumbered us and the fight was hard, however this time we were sure to win…"

Orm made a pause, emptied a cup of mead and wiped his gray mustache with the back of his hand.

"And so it happened. We sank two of their boats and captured three; the last one ran for its life, and as the night fell, we didn't bother following it. That was when we found that Torgeir lay unconscious.

"Torgeir was covered in his own blood and the wound in his left side was so deep and bad, that none of us could understand how he had managed to fight with us during those last hours, giving orders with his usual energy and determination…" the old man averted his glance and sighed heavily. As he went on, his voice became dull.

"We knew he had no chance, but he came back to his senses and spoke. He gave us orders, precise and wise, and we followed every one of them.

"First, he wanted us to keep going until we conquered an important strategic point, and we were to find one at the morning. Meanwhile, he ordered the ships to gather for the night. He stayed where he was, on the deck, his wounds covered with a tight bandage. Torgeir knew death stood by his side and spared himself unnecessary movements and suffering, but willed himself to stay alive for as long as possible. That very night he announced that he wanted us to return and name a new konungr, once our mission completed. He also wanted us to ask his beloved wife, Turid, not to sacrifice herself, but to live and help in choosing the new konungr, as well as to look after his sons."

Orm fell silent for several heartbeats and absently ran his hand up and down his face. His audience didn't move. They just sat there frozen, eyes fixed expectantly on the old story-teller.

"With the first rays of the dawn, we headed toward the Foreigners' land. We hoped to get to their main city, but instead, several miles short of it, we fell upon their fortress. It stood hidden between the rocks, and could only be seen once passed. At that time, Torgeir could barely speak. He looked at the fortress, and then gave us orders with his eyes closed.

"We attacked quickly and by surprise. The fight was fierce but short. The fortress fell. We lost nine people, while their dead tripled ours. Those who remained alive were kept as prisoners.

"Torgeir must have felt that moment. He fell unconscious since giving his last orders, living his last moments. But when Ari appeared on the top of the fortress wall, brandishing our flag, Torgeir opened his eyes and looked around with a long, wise glance; he looked for the last time, his eyes dark with pain. He looked at the clear blue sky, at the bright and warm rising sun, at the long golden pathway that its reflection formed on the moving surface of the sea; he looked at Ari, and as he looked, a smile lit his pale, exhausted face. That beautiful, happy and serene smile that does not belong to the world of the living…"

Orm took a deep breath and went on louder, trying to hide the deep emotions his voice betrayed.

"Torgeir was dead, but he died like a konungr, like a true hero, a man of exceptional courage and of rare strength… the man we will always remember and admire!"

The crowd roared unanimously, honoring the konungr.

"Before leaving the fortress, we made a worthy funeral

for our konungr in the biggest and finest foreign ship. We filled the ship with gold and jewels from the fortress, we brought there the best weapons and food and animals, so that Torgeir was ready to travel to Valhalla. We sang for Torgeir's glory as we pushed the ship away from the shore and lit it with our torches. As the fire burned higher and stronger, a blast of strong wind caught the ship, propelling her toward the setting sun.

"Our konungr was gone as a true hero, brave, strong and generous. He was a good man and a fair ruler and Odin welcomed him in Valhalla where he now feasts with Gods and with those of his crew who died in this battle."

While Orm spoke, Turid sat motionless. She saw every scene he was describing as if she was there; she felt the salty wind on her skin and experienced all Torgeir's pain as her own. It felt like sharp blades slowly cutting into her flesh. There was nothing she could have done for him. He died on a foreign land, far from home, and she was denied even a final farewell. Through Orm's words, Turid watched her husband draw his final breath. Watching his exhausted beautiful face and his last smile, Turid felt something die inside her. One tear ran down her cheek and fell down on her skirt, but she could not allow herself to cry. She was a queen and she had to act with dignity. Crying was considered a weakness. Turid fought her pain and despair with all her might. She bit the inside of her cheek and clenched her fists as tight as she could.

People started singing to honor the konungr and all the dead. Turid took a rasping breath and joined them. Her voice was weak and quivering at first, but as the song went on it became easier, as if some of her pain was getting out with the sound. By the end of the song she was in control of her emotions enough to be able to finish the ceremony with dignity. And even though she saw everything from afar, through the curtain of pain, her voice was even and her posture straight and proud, as needed.

Olaf and Hrafn felt just as bad: for boys to weep was even more shameful than for the most high-ranked women. Having to suppress it was a real torture. In addition, even though they were positive now that their mother wouldn't sacrifice herself, they worried about her. They watched her every movement anxiously and prayed to all the gods to help her. They stayed with her until the very end of the ceremony and felt relieved when they were finally able to go home.

But even at home they remained silent, too exhausted and shocked to exchange words. Neither knew what to say.

When they got home, Ari knocked on the door. He brought with him Torgeir's sword and carefully deposited it on the bench.

"Torgeir ordered me to give his sword to the next konungr. He chose to go to Valhalla with his spears," he explained quietly.

His words met no particular reaction, so he remained silent for a while, absently scratching his head. Then he swallowed and muttered, "His last words were that he loves all of you more than anything… and wants all of you to live happily, taking care of each other and our people…" Ari's voice betrayed him and he had to clench hard both his fists to fight the coming tears.

In front of him, the queen and her sons sat close together on the straw mats. They were quiet and distant. None of them touched the konungr's sword, as if they were scared to do so.

Ari was Torgeir's closest friend, they grew up, played, and then fought together, and Torgeir's death was very painful for him. However, Ari felt helpless in front of Turid's silent despair. He could think of nothing else to tell them, so he went away, leaving them alone with their pain.

~~~

With the first roosters' crowing the dead konungr's uncle Folke knocked on their door. He found the queen sitting by the nearly extinguished fire. Her sons were curled up by her side, fast asleep.

The man greeted her with a bow. Turid nodded in response and pressed a finger to her lips. Folke understood and noiselessly stepped out of the longhouse.

Turid joined him and silently closed the door behind her, trying to not wake the boys.

Just as the door closed, Hrafn opened his eyes and sat up. His twin woke as well, but, feeling very sleepy, just gave Hrafn a brief glance and closed his eyes again.

Fast and silent like a wild cat, Hrafn got to the door and pressed his ear against it.

"Forgive me, queen, for bothering you when your grief is so great…" the man said hesitantly, "… but the council needs to talk to you."

Turid didn't answer, but apparently she nodded or somehow encouraged the man, for he went on.

"Important decisions are to be made and time is short. Our people need a new konungr, and we believe that you are the one to guide us in our choice…"

Turid's voice was calm and serious when she replied, "I understand. Take me to the assembly. As for the boys, let them sleep. They need it after what have happened."

Footsteps told Hrafn that both were gone. He went back to his place by the fire. Olaf opened one eye.
~~~

"They are going to name the konungr," Hrafn informed him.

"What are we going to do?"

Hrafn sat down, closed his eyes and answered, "For now we can sleep. We will know if anything interesting happens soon enough."

This time, his twin didn't even open an eye. "Mmm… wake me up…"

"I will," whispered Hrafn and lay down. Comfortably stretching his body, he adjusted his sheep-fur blanket and closed his eyes.

The Choice

The council was held in the great hall in the center of the town. It was not yet the voting assembly. Only jarls were there, sitting in a circle.

Torgeir's uncle opened the door and stepped aside to let Turid pass. The elders of the council stood to greet her.

The woman greeted them back and took a seat among them in the circle.

Harald, the eldest presiding over the assembly, spoke first.

"Thank you, queen, for acting so soon. We sincerely admire your strength and devotion to our people."

Turid just nodded. She knew they meant it, but she felt nothing special about her deed.

Harald went on. "Konungr Torgeir was our love and pride. He ruled wisely and died heroically. He will live forever in our hearts and songs… but now, a new chieftain must be named, for a lot of important decisions must be made. The war is not over."

Turid nodded again. She wanted to hear it all before saying anything.

Harald seemed to understand her strategy. His eyes sparkled and a light smile touched his lips, making his long mustache move up.

"As both of your sons are only ten-winters-old, we have a difficult choice. We believe your advice is necessary here, for you have been a wise and devoted queen.

"There are only two possible solutions: someone rules until your eldest son Olaf is twelve-winters-old, or we name Olaf our konungr, even though he is still too young. We believe only two people entitled to take the rule instead of your son—you or Örjan, Torgeir's brother.

"We ask for your choice and will then vote," he concluded, looking at the young woman.

Turid stared at the ground, thinking. She knew something like this was coming, yet he didn't enlighten her about the answer she should give. Of one thing she was sure—she was unable to become a war leader. Bloody battles were her worst gut-wrenching fear that never eased. It had taken her years to learn to keep a controlled expression when somebody was even talking about it, and ever since her husband decided to go to war, she was having horrible nightmares.

As for Örjan, he looked much more like a peaceful farmer than a chieftain. Yet it seemed wise discussing it with him before deciding.

Then she pictured her son Olaf who was now peacefully sleeping at home. Tall, good-looking and fair-haired, he was quick and smart, and rather good in fighting, just like his brother. They looked absolutely identical; the only thing allowing their mother to tell Olaf from Hrafn was the color of their eyes. Olaf's were gray, turning nearly black when he was upset or very excited, while Hrafn's were of that rare deep emerald green that fascinated anyone who looked into them. The twins were best friends and both promised to become great warriors.

On the other hand, they were only boys, her boys, and taking from one of them two winters of quiet childhood seemed cruel.

At the same time, the future of her people was at stake.

Turid tried to imagine her son as a konungr, looking for some sort of hint, for some indication that would give her the right answer. She knew she had to be very careful, for many destinies were in her hands.

But the more she thought, the more baffled she felt. Sighing heavily, she looked up at the council participants and said what seemed the most appropriate, given the situation.

"Honored council, I do understand the urgency of the matter. However, I would like to remind you that the issue is very important, for I am deciding not only the destiny of my children, but of all our people. I do not refuse this responsibility, but I would like to think it over and to talk about it to the others concerned."

People around her listened, their expressions guarded, and Turid felt that they were reluctant to postpone the decision. All right then, she would give them a concession, because it seemed the only way to get what she wanted.

She added, "You'll have my answer by sunset."

Several faces around her visibly relaxed, while Harald and a couple of others remained expressionless. Turid felt that this time, she had it her way.

The confirmation came immediately.

"So be it," said Harald, and the rest of the council openly agreed with him.

~~~

First, Turid went to see Örjan. She knew him to be an honest, simple and extremely shy person, and she decided that his opinion might be useful anyway.

Örjan and his family lived in the neighboring village, and Turid rode there.
~~~

When she arrived, it was already midday. She found Örjan leaving his field for his meal. Obviously, he did not expect to see her.

"Sorry for interrupting, but I must speak with you," she announced, jumping off her horse.

Strong, tall and muscled, just like her dead husband, Örjan had bright red hair, and his nearly colorless eyes made his face look unexpressive. He scratched his head, not really knowing what to say.

Turid addressed him an encouraging smile and stopped outside the fence, giving him some space and a chance to overcome his shyness.

Örjan took a deep breath and finally said, "I did not expect to see you so soon after... well... what happened. But I'm glad you came. Please come and be my guest."

His sincerity made her feel better.

"Thank you for your hospitality," she answered. "But my time is very short. If you don't mind, I'll just talk here and go."

The man nodded, and Turid quickly told him about the request of the council.

Örjan's clear eyes rolled in amazement. "That's impossible! ... Me? A konungr?" he chuckled bitterly. "Can you see me ruling?"

Turid did not reply. She wanted to hear his mind and she knew that even a slightest intervention would doom the intent.

Looking away, he stepped toward her and laid his huge, calloused hand on the fence between them. He remained like that, staring at the ground, before finally meeting Turid's gaze. He shook his head and said, "I am flattered, but you know it: I'm not like my brother. I'm a farmer, and I'm happy with that."

There was so much pain and sorrow in his eyes that they turned gray. Stunned, Turid discovered for the first time the deep and sincere love and admiration Örjan felt for his brother. It was so unexpected and touching, that tears filled her eyes.

Örjan looked away, leaning against the wooden fence.

"I just… don't think I will be a good chieftain for our people," he confessed, and seized his head with both hands.

"I have always been too bad at planning, and then…" Turid could see how uncomfortable and ashamed he felt making such a confession, "…with my illness, I don't think I'll be able to bear such a responsibility," he finished in a whisper.

Turid felt very bad for having made him talk of it—ever since his early childhood, Örjan had uncontrollable fits when facing a stressful situation. Few people knew it, for his family and close friends protected him as much as they could, and it was difficult to suspect given Örjan's colossal size and muscles.

Leaning against the fence next to him, Turid put her hand on his shoulder. "It wasn't my intention to force you into anything," she gently reassured him. "I just needed your opinion."

The man slowly nodded and lowered his hands.

"I miss him terribly," he confessed, still looking down.

Turid swallowed, trying to chase away the upcoming tears, and gently stroke his red hair. "We all miss him…"

Örjan suppressed a sob before regaining the control of his emotions. Giving Turid a guilty smile, he said, "Sorry, I'm the one who should be consoling you."

The woman chuckled bitterly and looked away. "In grief we are all the same."

They remained silent for a while, both thinking of

Torgeir, of what a wonderful man he was and of all those moments they were lucky to have shared with him.

Turid broke the silence first. "If I may ask you only one more thing, just between us… Who do you think is now the most suitable for succession?"

For several long moments, Örjan remained silent, watching a raven soar over the edge of the forest. Finally, he turned to look at Turid.

"I think, Hrafn," he said quietly, to the woman's utmost surprise.

She rolled her eyes at him. "But he is the youngest!"

Örjan shrugged and looked down, confused. "Well, it's just my opinion…" he muttered.

~~~

On her way back, Turid kept hurrying her horse. Her discussion with Örjan left her even more confused. Before there were three potential candidates: Olaf, Örjan and herself, but now her youngest son Hrafn was brought into it. She was irritated and disappointed. She expected a good piece of advice from Örjan, because he knew her twins rather well, and both boys loved him. But Örjan picked none of the three possible. Was he trying to escape the need to make a decision not to offend anyone? Or did he really think that Hrafn was the best to rule? Well, there was no way for Hrafn to become the next konungr—the tradition demanded the eldest to take the father's place. And Hrafn was born right after Olaf.

But no matter what, she had to choose. The day was inexorably fading. She felt panic growing inside of her.

There still was one more way to avoid any possible
~~~

mistake. The surest and the most objective. Turid did not want to do it, but she had no other solution. Praying to all the gods, she turned her horse toward the forest.

~~~

Olaf and Hrafn were cutting wood with a couple of other boys. Hrafn stopped and pulled his brother by the hand.

"Olaf," he whispered. "Mother went to see the rune caster!"

Olaf didn't bother to put a shirt. "We'll be right back!" he threw to the other boys who exchanged surprised looks, and the twins ran away as fast as they could.
~~~

The Rune Caster

Just like her dead husband, Turid believed that the future was not meant to be known in advance. She lived day by day, facing whatever was to come and listening to her intuition. However, this time she was lost and confused, and her intuition fell silent at the thought that she was to determine the future of several towns.

The decision to see the rune caster was not an easy one. She felt guilty, she felt like she was cheating, and several times she nearly turned back.

When she finally knocked at the door of the rune caster's hut, her heart was heavy.

The rune caster greeted her warmly, and politely offered her a cup of rich-smelling herbal tea.

He was a tall, bony man with long, white hair and beard. His face was long and thin, and so were his delicate white fingers. Despite his isolated way of living, he was known for his constant good mood and his love of a good jest. He always wore beautifully colored clothes, and many bright, colorful cushions decorated his simple hut.

With sincere and touching care, the old man gathered a pile of cushions on the floor by the fireplace for Turid and made sure she was comfortable. Then he sat on the floor in front of her and drank his tea in silence, smiling comfortingly and not asking her anything.

Inhaling the aroma of her herbal tea, Turid did not speak either. She was surprised but grateful for his hospitality, and relaxed a bit.

She slowly finished her tea and finally spoke. "Forgive me, ellri[*], for bothering you. I have an important decision to make and I feel I am lost..."

The rune caster slightly nodded, encouraging her. His amber eyes shone with attention.

Turid drew a deep breath, and went on. "As you probably know, my husband is dead, but the war is not over. The Foreign king is already gathering his army to invade more of our lands. We need a konungr to lead our people in this war and to grant us unity and prosperity after. The council is waiting for my opinion, but I'm not sure any of us is good enough."

The old man took a sip of tea and put his cup away. "It will be my pleasure to help you, even though I see you don't feel good about what you are asking."

Turid blushed under his kind but penetrating gaze.

"I will cast the runes for you and will tell you what the gods advise you to do..."

He stood and retrieved his small leather bag with runes from a wooden trunk.

Back to his seat in front of the young woman, he opened it and carefully checked every rune stone. Then he put them back into the bag, closed his eyes, and fell silent. He concentrated his thoughts on Turid's problem.

To Turid, it all seemed incredible. With a mixture of dull worry and childish curiosity, she observed the old man, not suspecting that her sons held their breath, pressing their ears to the door from outside.

---

[*] Ellri—elder (Old Norse)

The rune caster shook the bag, making the runes click and jump inside, and muttering to himself. Then he turned it upside down and emptied it on the floor in front of him. He thoughtfully studied the rectangular stones, then spoke. "Your eldest son and a regent received the same number of votes. That's why the council left the final decision for you."

Turid nodded.

"You can't resolve yourself to rule because you are afraid of the war. You have lost family in battle and you fear that you will not be able to send someone else to death."

The young woman's face turned bright red. She was suddenly frightened of this strange old man who revealed so easily her deepest and most shameful secrets.

But the rune caster smiled kindly. "I'm not here to judge you, nor do I believe that weaknesses are shameful…

"You brother-in-law refused to reign as well… He is honest and his decision is wise…

"Your sons remain…"

He sighed. Then, without looking at Turid, he reached for his cup and took a long sip of tea.

Outside, the boys exchanged excited looks, pressing their ears even harder against the wooden door.

"Your eldest boy is named 'ancestors' descendant'. A good name for a good konungr. He will be a strong and wise leader. People will remember him as Olaf the Fair. He will bring to life the projects of his brother. He will have eight sons and live a long, happy life, until death takes him, and his eldest son will take his place as a konungr…"

A broad grin lit Olaf's face. His brother's face returned his happy grin as Hrafn noiselessly patted his shoulder, congratulating him.

A weak smile touched Turid's lips. She had pride for her son, yet she couldn't help feeling this ordeal was not over.

"As for battles, Olaf will win only one. He will avenge his brother…"

With a dull thud, Turid's cup fell on the floor. The noise made the twins jump, but they instantly regained their position.

The rune caster stopped, gathered the fallen cup and stood. Moving deliberately slowly, he rinsed it, poured more tea for Turid, and patiently waited for her to drink. Only then did he sit back and continue.

"With the help of a woman, Olaf will conquer a large, rich foreign country and our people will rule over it forever, until their race disappears completely."

He stopped and seemed to ponder his next question for a while.

"Why did you call the second boy 'raven'? There was no man called so before…"

Turid's voice was weak and unsure when she answered.

"After he was born, a raven flew into the room and sat next to him. I got scared and wanted to chase the bird, but my son held his hand toward it and the bird bowed as if blessing him. My husband said it was a sign. Since then, the raven has always been around, keeping a close eye on my son."

"Oh… I see," muttered the old man. "Now I understand."

The twins exchanged worried looks: did the old man see that Hrafn and his raven were really one, that they shared thoughts and feelings? But the old man did not explain and instead heaved a sigh and went on with his prophecy.

"The Raven boy has wisdom and a rare inner strength. He is smart and creative. He will be a very good Viking. He will taste the utmost happiness, for he will find his true love. She is a foreign princess. But they will soon lose each other.

Their union is doomed… I see Raven failing... A choice is to be made: one will die, while the other will stay in this world, neither dead nor alive. They will be separated forever. Centuries of unbearable pain and suffering lay in front of him…" ·

Turid's face went bloodless. A loving mother's heart is seldom mistaken—she felt something was to go wrong. Legends said that true love was the greatest happiness a living person could experience. But once found, it should not be lost, or both would suffer. No remedy would help them, for after they have known what it felt like to share a soul, they can no longer stay apart.

Turid, who had just lost her beloved husband, knew how painful it was. But if the legends were true, her son's pain would be even worse. Her heart bled at the thought of her boy having such a terrible fate.

Behind the door, the twins exchanged stunned looks.

Not letting her dwell on sad thoughts, the rune caster concluded, "Both of your sons are made to be great konungrs. They have their father's temper. You should be proud of them.

"Now that I told you what you needed to know, you'd better go and get ready for the ceremony. People await your decision."

The young woman gave him a puzzled look.

But the rune caster nodded and waved her to approach. Bending so close that his beard tickled her cheek, he whispered something in her ear.

The Ceremony

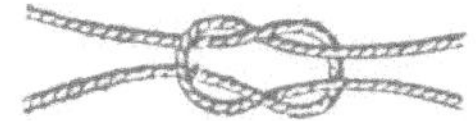

At sunset, the members of the council and all those who were able to come gathered in the vast clearing in front of the great hall.

Washed and dressed in a hurry, Olaf and Hrafn stood there as well. They had to run back from the rune caster's hut and didn't have time to exchange their thoughts, which made their waiting nearly unbearable. Both had a hard time staying in place, for both itched to talk it over privately. At the same time, the ceremony was too important to miss, especially given the real possibility of Olaf being proclaimed the new chieftain. So they burned with impatience.

Örjan, his wife, and his daughters stood next to them. Örjan was probably even more nervous than his nephews: he honestly feared what was about to happen. All the more, he had never liked being the center of attention. He slouched, shifting from one foot to the other, his gaze fixed upon the ground. He felt that his desire to flee was too obvious, and it made him burn with shame.

Jarls, warriors, farmers, free workers, and slaves from their town and from the neighboring villages gathered around, curious to know the name of the new konungr. Excited whispers came from all sides; all the attention was focused on their small group, making them feel oddly and unpleasantly apart.

Finally, Turid appeared, and the crowd almost instantly fell silent. The tension in the air became almost perceptible as the young woman made her way to the center of the circle. She looked tired and older, her long fair hair tied into a knot, and the corners of her lips bent downward. A few steps behind her walked the old rune caster. He wore his best embroidered blue shirt, and a belt decorated with silver and precious stones over his leather trousers.

At his sight, the twins exchanged alarmed looks.

The old man took a place among the crowd, as if he was merely part of the curious audience and not an active participant. He greeted everybody with a nod, then glanced at the twins and suddenly winked.

The boys stiffened, staring at the old man, but then Turid spoke, and they instantly forgot about the rune caster.

Turid greeted the crowd and fell silent, obviously gathering her thoughts. There was something alarming about her tense and pained expression.

Their feelings sharpened by curiosity, people around her froze suddenly aware of the fact that their destiny was being decided.

The young queen drew a deep, silent breath and people around her did the same.

"Honorable assembly," she finally began. "This very morning, I was asked to suggest the successor to my husband, Konungr Torgeir, who died defeating the enemy in a fierce battle, yet not finishing the war."

Her posture was proud and her voice was calm and clear, but the twins felt that it demanded a lot of effort from her.

"I know my suggestion will affect the future of our people and the outcome of the war. This is why I decided not to stop at my own opinion, but to talk to several people, including the rune caster."

The crowd muttered in approval—the rune caster was highly respected. No one doubted his prophecies, for all of them had come true.

Turid continued.

"The glory and prosperity of our people have always been and are my primary concern. With that, I suggest to name as our next konungr my son…"

Olaf's eyes sparkled with pride and excitement and Hrafn turned to look at him, drawing a deep breath to shout his congratulations first.

"…Hrafn," finished Turid, and though her voice remained even, it sounded rather like a groan of hidden pain.

Hrafn froze, his mouth open and his lungs so full with air that they threatened to explode. It couldn't be! He must have misheard! But the bewildered look on his brother's face told him that he was not the only one.

Then the moment of silent shock was over and uproar broke from the crowd around them.

"That's impossible! …"

"He's the youngest!"

"That's wrong!"

"The eldest boy must rule!"

Turid stood motionless, praying it would end soon.

The rune caster was silent, observing the scene.

Örjan was relieved. He happily patted Hrafn's shoulder in sign of sincere congratulation and beamed.

Hrafn blinked and remembered to breathe. He glanced at Olaf, whose shock quickly turned into vivid anger. Hrafn shook his head in an instinctive attempt to get rid of such a misunderstanding.

But Olaf seemed to take it seriously. A frown twisting his face, he pointed his finger at his brother and shouted, "That's not fair! I was born first, everyone knows it!"

This undeserved anger felt like a painful slap, like a treachery. Hrafn wanted to retort, but the pain of this sudden outburst left him speechless.

"Silence!" Harald's powerful voice boomed over the uproar.

As if by magic, everyone fell silent and looked at him.

"All of you know that the assembly must vote on every proposal before it becomes a law," he announced angrily. "According to the tradition, the person who made the proposal has the right to defend it. So now, I suggest everyone to close their mouth and open their ears. We will listen to what our queen has to tell us."

All the eyes turned to Turid again. She threw a quick glance at the rune caster, as if looking for help, and swallowed hard.

"I do honestly think, and Örjan here agreed with me, that my sons are better suited to rule than me or him. As for the last choice, the rune caster suggested it to me."

Everyone, including Turid, looked at the rune caster. The latter calmly stepped forward and spoke for the first time.

"Honorable assembly, I have been living among you for more than fifty winters now, and nearly everyone here has come at least once to seek my advice. You know better than I whether my prophecies have been wrong."

The people muttered in agreement.

"So today, at our queen's request, I cast the runes for the boys. Both are destined to be good konungrs. I am not to reveal what fates the gods have for them, but one thing made me suggest the youngest as the successor: the Raven boy is the only one who will win the present war."

The crowd gasped.

"I will say no more," finished the rune caster. "Now vote, and may Odin guide you."

With that he stepped back and crossed his arms over his chest.

People were obviously confused. They argued until night fall but finally gave their votes.

The rune caster's arguments had their effect: the vast majority voted for Hrafn because they wanted victory in the war. The opposition clung to the traditions, but took their defeat quiet peacefully, without furious yells and menaces.

Harald walked toward Hrafn, who still wore a flabbergasted expression, and put his hand on the boy's shoulder.

"By the honest vote of the assembly I declare Hrafn, son of Torgeir, our new konungr!"

Most of the people yelled in approval.

Harald waited for them to calm down and went on. "Let us celebrate now. And tomorrow, after the sun rises…" there he looked down at Hrafn and went on with a challenging spark in his eyes, "…we will start the preparations for war."

Hrafn swallowed and nodded. A sudden fear started growing inside him.

Harald's brow wrinkled slightly, betraying his skepticism, but he said nothing.

In the next moment, Hrafn was separated from him as the crowd hurried toward the long row of wooden tables, already groaning with food and drinks. The feast began.

Hrafn sat alone at the head of the table. His raven was back with him—after having informed Hrafn that his mother went to see the rune caster, the bird joined him there and then flew back to the village with him. Now the raven was perched on the back of his tall, wooden chair. From his place, Hrafn could see nearly everyone and, most importantly, was seen by everyone, which made him feel rather awkward.

Obviously still angry with him, Olaf had Ari sit between them. As for Turid, she sat at Hrafn's left, next to Örjan and his family. Örjan's wife, Aud, an opposite of her shy husband, was already overwhelming Turid with gossip, managing to eat and talk at the same time.

Hrafn felt isolated and avoided, as if he had become different from everybody. He found it unpleasant and had to struggle to keep smiling and answering politely to questions and congratulations. His heart heavy, he didn't feel like eating or drinking, and fortunately people kept talking to him, preventing him from doing so.

As for his brother, Olaf ate and drank enough for both. Rare were the occasions when ten-winter-olds were allowed to drink, so Olaf took advantage of the situation, emptying his second cup of mead.

The feast went on as usual: after eating, people began singing and dancing in the fire light.

Normally keen on dancing, Hrafn danced only one dance with one of his cousin and left. He could no longer stand this misunderstanding and the resulting feeling of loneliness, and decided to talk to the closest people he had: his mother and his brother.

The latter obviously had had his dose of mead—drunk asleep, he had fallen backwards off the bench. He lay on the grass, his mouth open and his arms spread wide on his sides, as if waiting for a hug.

Hrafn couldn't suppress a chuckle. If only they were friends like before, he would have made a joke out of it, but now it seemed out of place. With a sigh, the new king bent down and seizing his brother by the armpits, heaved him on the bench, so that no one would walk or fall over him.

"Looks like the new konungr is the only one still sober," he heard Ari's loud voice behind him and turned.

The warrior smiled down at him. In the light of recent events, Ari seemed more strong and mighty, and next to him Hrafn felt small and childish. Not knowing what to say to not appear ridiculous, the boy just shrugged.

"Good for you," commented Ari, eyeing Olaf's body. "You don't need a dull head tomorrow."

Hrafn stiffened. Why were all of them talking about tomorrow? He had a vague idea of what was about to happen then and the expectant allusions everyone kept making about it made the boy dread it.

Ari had drunk a lot, but he was used to it, for his brain was quite clear.

"Can we talk at the morning?" Hrafn asked, hoping it would ease his growing anxiety.

"Of course." replied the warrior. "Come to the ship at the dawn." He stopped, realizing that he was speaking to the king now, and it was not appropriate for him to command like that.

Hrafn understood and hurried to accept. "I'll be there. It's the best place."

Both remained silent for a while, not knowing what to say.

Ari moved first. Pointing at Olaf, he muttered, "I'll take him home. It's cold outside in the morning."

Hrafn nodded. "Yes, please..."He watched Ari lift his brother's limp body from the bench and carry him away with such ease as if Olaf weighed no more than a cat.

Then, Hrafn looked for his mother, but she was nowhere to be seen. The little voice inside his head told him that there was something wrong with it, but he rejected that idea, too willing to think that she was busy.

Instead, he spotted the rune caster who was leaving. Hrafn hurried after him.

"Ellri! Ellri! Please, wait! "

The old man heard and stopped, patiently waiting for the boy to approach.

Suddenly Hrafn felt lost for words. He wanted to ask so many things, yet didn't know what to say or where to start.

"Why?" he managed to mumble finally. He wanted to say that he had not heard anything about the present war in the prophecy, but stopped just in time, ashamed of their spying.

The old man seemed to know his thoughts, for his amber eyes sparkled with amusement.

"I understand your curiosity, young man," he said, smiling. "That's why I revealed some details that your mother doesn't necessarily need to know yet..."

"Oh." Hrafn felt from the beginning that the rune caster knew of their spying, but hearing it from him was strange.

"...but now I think you've heard enough."

Hrafn opened his mouth to contradict, but the rune caster interrupted him by lifting his hand.

"You know the main path of your destiny now, but it's still up to you to craft it. You don't want to live like a dog following its master's whims, do you?"

Hrafn shook his head. Not that he felt sure of it, but that was what the old man expected him to do.

"A man of wisdom faces it all and makes choices that can change many things. Don't you agree?"

Puzzled, the boy opened his mouth and closed it, defeated. Unable to hide his disappointment, he nodded. He could not disagree with the old man, but he had hoped so much to hear something reassuring. Instead, he felt lonely and helpless.

Even if the rune caster read his thoughts, this time he did not react. He only patted the boy's shoulder and said,

"Use *your* strength, but always remember that any strength may become a weakness."

Hrafn raised his brows in surprise, just like his father used to do, but the old man smiled and added, "Good luck to you, Konungr Raven, and may Thor help you!"

With that he was gone.

Hrafn remained motionless for a moment, his heart heavy. With a deep sigh, he slowly headed home.

As he reached the door, the big black raven flew toward him and landed on his shoulder. The boy thoughtfully stared at the bird, and after some hesitation, turned on his heels and headed toward the dark forest.

King's First Decision

When the sun's first rays gently touched the waking earth, Hrafn was washed and dressed, heading toward the sea. His raven was perched on his shoulder.

The town around them was just waking, birds and other animals rended the dawn silence, but people remained in their beds. It was usual to get up later after feasts.

Glad not to meet anyone, the young boy walked past the great hall where he had been proclaimed king. Reminding him of the feast, the ground was covered with litter and cut flowers, there were several overthrown cups and even someone's forgotten shoe. Yesterday's events seemed absolutely impossible in the morning. Hrafn realized that things were never going to be the same for him. His careless childhood was over. Now he had to lead people to the war and to win where his father died. Only his father had been a great Viking and an experienced sailor, while he, Hrafn, had never killed in his life.

Hrafn walked to the water and stopped several yards from the docks. He stretched out his arm. The raven hopped on it and turned to face the boy. They stared at each other for a while, silently talking. Then the boy managed a weak smile and whispered, "Yes, we'll do our best."

The bird croaked in agreement and took off. It had a new mission: it was flying forward to assess the situation and warn Hrafn of the enemy's plans. They had decided it together at night and Hrafn only hoped the raven would have enough time to do it. But as the bird was now his only friend, Hrafn couldn't help feeling insecure watching it fly away.

The raven made a circle above the boy and soared over the waves, toward the horizon.

Hrafn watched his raven until it disappeared. Left alone, he felt worry creeping back inside him, but there was no going back. He had always dreamt of becoming a great Viking and here was his chance to do so. He filled his lungs with fresh morning air and clenched his fists. He had to be strong and calm. He had to inspire respect and fear, just as his father had done.

Straightening his back, he exhaled and walked toward the docks.

The ships stood empty and motionless, their oars care-fully stowed and their sails down. The crews slept on dry land. Ari was there, keeping his promise. He waved to the boy and helped him to get on the ship.

"You haven't slept," he stated after a brief glance at Hrafn's red, swollen eyes.

"Nor have you," retorted the boy. "Was it hard standing guard after the feast?"

Ari chuckled in his beard and shrugged.

"I'm used to it. How're you feeling?"

"I am well," reassured the boy.

They stood silent for a moment, Hrafn thoughtfully looking around and Ari just scratching his beard. Then the boy spoke. "Look, I have never sailed yet, so will you please show me around before the others come?"

A broad grin lit the giant's face. "With pleasure…"

An hour later, when the warriors finally gathered by the

ship, Ari was showing Hrafn how he had saved Torgeir from the Foreign boat.

"I tied the rope to my belt here," he said. "This way, I was able to use both my hands. Watch!" taking a couple of steps backwards, he ran and jumped.

The mast slightly cracked as the giant took off the deck and made a large circle in the air, before landing back nearly at the same place.

Hrafn watched with his mouth open.

"Hey, Ari," called a warrior named Kirk. "We all have something more important to do than to admire your old deeds!"

Some Vikings laughed and Ari went pink.

"I asked him to do so," Hrafn said firmly.

The laughter stopped at once and an awkward silence fell.

Everyone glared at him. Surrounded by those tall, strong warriors who had been his father's crew and army, Hrafn felt small and helpless. How could he dare give orders to those mighty and experienced giants? Even if he dared, they would never listen to a child! His stomach shrank with fear and he fought a strong urge to run away. It was impossible. He had no choice. Badly needing to say something, Hrafn asked the first thing that came to his mind.

"Can somebody tell me again what exactly my father's last orders were?"

His question was met by silence. A couple of warriors skeptically twisted their lips. As Hrafn wasn't addressing someone in particular, no one felt concerned enough to answer.

A warrior named Sveinn finally spoke.

"Torgeir wanted us to have a strategic point conquered, and we took a fortress. One of our ships and forty people stayed there."

"Why is that fortress important?"

Sveinn shrugged. "Well, it's quiet far from their towns and looks pretty isolated."

"It is still a coastal protection," said Ari. "It is well fortified and there were many weapons inside."

Hrafn nodded thoughtfully. It seemed to him important enough to find out the real use of the conquered fortress for the Foreigners.

"My father asked you to go back here and return with more people?" he asked, this time talking directly to Ari.

Ari thoughtfully scratched his beard. "Well... he didn't give clear instructions for that. He said the new konungr has to be named as soon as possible, and then *he* will decide," he shrugged. "So it's up to you."

Silence fell once again. Hrafn tried to imagine what his father could have meant in his orders. He was sure there was some hidden sense in them. He had spent the whole night thinking of it and discussing it all with his raven, and there was one important thing that he understood.

Ever since he and Olaf were four-winter-old, their father taught them how to wield different weapons. Olaf had inherited Torgeir's talent for spears while he, Hrafn, was better with the sword. With death standing at his side, Torgeir must have had some sort of premonition: he acted against the tradition, ordering them to send him to Valhalla with his spears instead of his sword. He had sent his sword to his successor as a gift and as a sign, obviously knowing who it would be.

Kirk's angry voice abruptly pulled him from his thoughts.

"For how long are we going to dwell on Torgeir's memory? We are at war and the enemy is not waiting!" He put his fists on his hips. "I understand all that kingship story, but men, let's face the reality!"

Straightening his back, he cast a heavy, challenging look at everyone, stopping at Hrafn, whose heart sank.

"The war is not a game for children. Foreigners not only outnumber us, but they have proved themselves to be good warriors. We need skills and experience to win!"

Hrafn knew just too well what Kirk was meaning. His worst fears were coming true. He felt hurt and humiliated. He would forever remember this shameful moment: strong, proud and angry Kirk towering over his small and weak figure, and all the Vikings watching in silence.

Kirk went on, pointing his finger at the boy.

"Here is my advice to you, Konungr: chose a warrior among us and let him lead us to war, before the damage is beyond repair!"

Several Vikings muttered in approval.

Hrafn averted his gaze, desperately trying to fight back treacherous tears. He knew Kirk was right, but delegating the command to another, and thus avoiding the responsibility for which he was chosen was cowardly. At the same time, he was taught to always think of what was best for his people, and to value life very highly. So, however miserable and heartbroken he was feeling, he resolved to pass the command on. Not to Kirk, but to Ari. Ari had been his father's best friend and a very good warrior.

All this flashed in his mind in the time of one breath. Wandering in the forest with only his raven for company, he had already thought of it. He drew a deep breath, trying to make his voice cold.

But before he could say a word, Orm hurried forward, scowling with anger. "What are you talking about?" he snapped at Kirk. "The boy has been voted konungr and it's no longer up to you to decide whether he is able to lead us to the war!"

"It's obvious, isn't it?" retorted Kirk.

Orm crossed his arms over his massive chest and lifted his chin. "If you are scared for your neck, you may stay home!"

Kirk's face went bright red and his clenched fists rose. "Me? Scared?!" he snarled, outraged, advancing on the storyteller.

"Stop it!" Ari yelled, stepping between them and pushing them away from each other with his both hands.

It took Kirk time to recover himself. Orm remained stiff and determined with his arms crossed over his chest.

Finally, Kirk threw an angry glance at Hrafn, stepped back and lowered his fists.

Then Ari spoke again. "I think Orm is right. The konungr should lead us. And we must help him out."

"We can win only if we are united, using the strength of all, and not leaving anyone behind!" added Orm.

Most of the warriors agreed. Kirk didn't look convinced, but he had nothing else to say. He just turned his back to everyone, staring at the sea. Orm threw a quick glance at Hrafn who was still fighting tears, and suggested, "Why don't we go and have a cooked meal on dry land? Haven't we been dreaming of it for weeks?"

"Aye!" agreed someone.

"Hot food!" said another.

"None for me," announced Sveinn. "Speak for yourself. I don't care about a hot morning meal on dry land unless it comes after an unforgettable night with a beautiful lass!"

Thunder-like guffaw shook the docks.

"Pretty maiden, keep me fed, I will warm for you your bed—" playfully sang someone and instantly several deep voices caught up with him as the warriors moved away from the ship.

"...Drink me drunk with your sweat mead—"

"I'll do anything you bid..."

"Sveinn, who was your lass last night?" asked a young, red-haired Viking.

Sveinn chuckled. "You'll get jealous if I tell you!"

"No way! No one is better than my Siv! ... So who was it?"

Ari approached the red-haired guy and gave him a heavy pat on the shoulder. "He's not telling you because it was your Siv!"

Everyone laughed again.

The red-haired jumped and vigorously shook his head. "No! It can't be! ... I was with her!"

"With her, or drunk, snoring at her feet?" teased someone, causing a new fit of laughter.

The red-head blushed furiously. He had been very drunk last night.

"C'mon, Sveinn, tell him! You're making him worry!" called someone through the laughter.

"Very well then," replied Sveinn. "It was Eydis, that charming beauty with generous hips and golden curls..."

Hrafn didn't feel like joining the laughter. He stood there motionless, watching them go. Orm put his hand on the boy's shoulder.

"Be strong, konungr. You'll do," he whispered and added with a wink, "And never cry in front of the warriors!"

With that, he left. Hrafn thought of joining them, but he didn't feel like eating. Staring at his own small shadow on the deck, he thought of Kirk, Orm, and the other warriors. No, he won't cry! He is the son of Konungr Torgeir the Brave! He will prove them he is worthy!

He straightened his back and looked around. Time was scarce and he was going to use all of it.

Realizing that he was left alone on the ship, he started carefully examining her on his own, recalling all the things Ari had told him. He even dove into the cold fiord water to inspect the keel. He had dreamed of commanding a warship like this.

Finally satisfied by his inspection of the ship, he got out of the water and headed for the beach.

Ari sat there, polishing his sword. He threw Hrafn an inquiring glance without pausing.

Hrafn threw back his wet hair and asked, "How much time do we need to get ready to sail?"

"No more than one day—the ships are not damaged. We only need arrows, provisions, and water."

The boy looked at the sea. "It takes seven days to get to the Foreigners in good weather…" he mused.

Hrafn frowned. He needed to discuss it with his raven. Their secret plan was to discover what the Foreigners were planning before taking any serious action. The bird was already flying to the Foreigners' mainland, but they needed some time. Hrafn closed his eyes and projected his thoughts to it.

He felt fresh, salty wind and saw the clear sky and the sparkling waves below. The freedom of flight was invigorating, but the raven listened attentively.

"The warriors don't want to linger," Hrafn explained silently.

"Try to get at least one day, otherwise it's worthless," the bird replied.

Hrafn opened his eyes and met Ari's gaze.

"One more day," he said. "Do you think we can spend one more day here?"

Ari shrugged and thoughtfully scratched his beard. "Well, it can be nothing or it can be vital… but others will accept it easier than if you wanted two more days."

Hrafn sighed. "Look, I really need it! Let's take the risk!"

The Viking looked hesitant, yet he made a weak nod. "As you wish, Konungr."

Hrafn nodded, too. "I need someone to draw a map of the Foreigners' land. As for the others, they may rest until tomorrow morning."

"I'll make a map, but first I have to go and tell them."

Ari strode away while Hrafn took off his shirt and squeezed the water out of it.

None of the warriors particularly appreciated the first order of the new konungr.

"The farce starts…" grumbled Kirk, gripping his belt.

"Orders are orders," Orm said calmly, but this time he sounded less convinced.

Ari shared their feelings. As a Viking and a warrior, he had a strong urge to do something, to join those who were left in the fortress, to go there and avenge Torgeir's death, or at least to start moving! Taking a rest at war time seemed unusual and shameful. On the other hand, as Torgeir's best friend, he didn't want to complicate even more the situation that was already pretty thorny, so he hurried to walk away, leaving his mates with their doubts.

The rest of the time before noon was spent by Ari and Hrafn on the beach. With a stick, Ari drew on the wet sand the plan of the Foreigners' land. It showed the big cavern where their first battle took place and the coast line, leading to the fortress.

"We didn't really have time to explore the rest," he explained.

Then Hrafn requested a plan of the fortress, asking questions about every step of their conquest and about everything they found inside.

Orm joined them to complete the missing pieces.

The boy seemed untiring, asking more and more questions about the Foreigners, their way of life, their traditions and gods. Soon both men didn't know what to say.

"Why do you need it anyway?" Ari asked with despair. "They are our enemies! We have to kill them instead of learning their ways!"

"I don't know yet," Hrafn confessed. "Anything can be useful…"

"He is right," Orm approved. "The more you know about your enemy, the easier it is fighting him."

Finally, Hrafn let both men go. Not that he had exhausted his large stock of questions, but they had told him all they knew. In addition, his stomach started rumbling loudly and he decided to go home and have a quick bite to eat.

He felt less miserable by now, but two important issues still had to be settled, for they burned him from inside, being the reason of most of his unease. He had to make peace with Olaf and to talk to their mother.

~~~

Coming to the house, he spotted Olaf in the yard and hurried toward him, eager to end it.

Olaf stood by the fence, clutching it with both hands, his back to his brother.

Hrafn strode toward him, purposefully making the grass rustle underfoot, so that Olaf would know he was there. But the latter didn't react.

"Olaf…" he began as he approached. "I need to talk to you…"

His brother slowly turned his head and looked at him. His
~~~

face was pale and swollen, and his eyes were bloodshot.

"I'm sick…" he muttered and proved it with action.

Hrafn grimaced, but didn't make a sound.

"I'll get you some water," he suggested once Olaf raised his head again.

As his brother wasn't showing any reaction at all, he seized a wooden bucket and ran to the well.

Olaf didn't move while he was away—he just stood there clutching the fence, his head down.

Hrafn brought back the bucket full of fresh cold water and at once poured it all over his brother's head.

Olaf gasped, taken aback, and once his voice was back, he glowered at Hrafn and grumbled, "What's that for?"

"To help you out." sheepishly shrugged his brother.

Olaf remained silent for a while, as if listening to his own body. Then he croaked, "Bring more!"

Hrafn repeated the procedure. This time Olaf didn't grumble, but put his swollen face under the fresh jet. Then he took a deep breath, released the fence and made a couple of uneven steps toward the wooden bench, on which he carefully lowered himself.

Hrafn joined him. For a little moment both remained silent. Then Olaf groaned, "My skull's going to explode!"

"Ari said you have to drink a cup of mead to feel better."

"Urgh!" groaned Olaf. "It will make me even sicker!"

Hrafn shrugged, "You better try. Seems like it's the only remedy."

Olaf leaned his back on the fence and closed his eyes.

"I'll go and get something to eat," offered Hrafn standing, but once again Olaf showed no reaction.

The boy brought some meat, cheese, and four fresh round loafs, together with a jar of mead and two wooden cups.

Olaf threw him a bleary glance through half-closed lids and said nothing.

Hrafn started eating. He was so hungry that the simple food was incredibly delicious. He was halfway through when Olaf groaned, "All right, give me some mead. Can't stand it anymore."

He dragged back his lids to look at his brother and straightened his back.

Hrafn filled the wooden cup with mead and put it into his brother's outstretched hand.

Olaf averted his head at the mere smell of it. Yet he forced himself to take a good gulp.

Hrafn stopped chewing, closely watching him.

Olaf's face screwed and twisted as if he had just swallowed an angry hedgehog. He covered his mouth with his hand, rolling his eyes, and took several deep breaths.

"How is it?" nearly whispered Hrafn, observing his brother with sincere concern.

"Huhumm…" was the answer that Hrafn interpreted as "Feels better, thanks," because Olaf just finished his cup and sighed in relief. He leaned back against the fence and closed his eyes again.

Hrafn assumed with disappointment that there would be no further conversation and resumed eating.

After some time, however, Olaf half opened his eyes and asked, "Gimme some bread, will you?"

He ate slowly and carefully, as if he was scared that his stomach wouldn't accept it. But that was not the case, and little by little, he finished the rest.

Then, without any further comment, he removed his wet shirt, stretched on the bench and fell fast asleep before his brother was able to decide what to say.

His back against the fence, Hrafn watched his brother,

puzzled. He was definitely not going to wake him up, especially after Olaf being that sick. So instead, he tried to think of something useful to do next. But it was not easy after eating: he started feeling tired and sleepy, and the midday warmth with the gentle breeze in the shade of the tree only made it worse.

It can't hurt sleeping for an hour or so, thought the boy, sliding from the bench and comfortably laying himself on the grass.

The Sword Fight

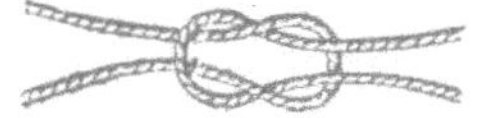

Hrafn didn't know how long he slept, but when he opened his eyes, it was early evening. Olaf glared at him from the bench with the bleary eyes of the freshly wakened.

Hrafn recalled the recent events and asked "Feel better?"

Olaf didn't answer straight away, but then he slowly lifted his head and moved to a sitting position.

"Guess the mead worked," he mumbled.

Hrafn grinned and moved to a sitting position as well. He was given a chance.

"There is something I need to tell you—" he began quickly, needing Olaf to listen and at the same time struggling to get his hoarse voice back to normal. "I swear to all gods I didn't do a thing to be named king! I was sure it had to be you and it just took me totally by surprise!"

He sighed; he didn't know what else to say to convince his brother.

Olaf blinked as if taken aback, and nodded.

Hrafn's eyes opened wide with surprise: he hadn't expected such a reaction.

Olaf averted his glance and started scratching the ground with the tip of his shoe. "I know." he muttered.

Hrafn swallowed hard, still not completely believing such a happy turn of the events. His eyes bright with hope, he asked, "So we are friends again?"

Olaf chewed his lip and then sheepishly met his gaze. "Yes."

Beaming, Hrafn offered him the outstretched little finger of his right hand.

Olaf seized it with his own little finger and they shook hands like that. The peace was made.

"Look, Olaf, I need to ask you something…"

"Go ahead," Olaf slid from the bench and sat on the grass next to his brother.

Hrafn chewed on the inside of his cheek, looking for the right words, and finally said, "All this succession story… It's just… I'm in more trouble than I could have imagined. They expect me to win the war, but it looks like the Foreigners outnumber us and I've never even fought for real! And the worst of it is that the Vikings will never take orders from me! For them I'm just a child—too young and too stupid. A lot of them really want me to step aside…"

Olaf looked thunderstruck. He did not expect in the slightest such a turn of the events.

Hrafn drew a deep breath and asked. "Do you feel like helping me?"

Olaf blinked, bemused.

"Well, together we are stronger, and if we could do it all together, it will be easier." Hrafn explained. "So what do you think? Are you with me?"

Olaf stared in disbelief. "You mean…" he mused, "you mean, we'll just share all together?"

Hrafn nodded, his expression serious.

A broad grin revealed all of Olaf's teeth. "I'm with you, brother."

~~~
~~~

An hour later, the twins practiced their fighting. They were used to doing it every day in their own yard, alternating bow, spears, and swords. Today it was swords and as they were friends again, there was no reason for missing it. Armed with two wooden swords and shields, the twins tried to come up with new blows and moves.

It went as usual. After an hour, a couple of other boys stopped by the fence, watching them, but the twins didn't pay attention, for they were accustomed to it.

When finally Hrafn defeated his brother for the third time and both were panting and sweaty, they decided to stop.

A man jumped over the fence and walked toward Olaf. Hrafn recognized Sveinn, the charmer Viking.

Sveinn held his hand toward Olaf's sword. "May I have that for a moment?"

Surprised, the boy just gave it to him.

Sveinn quickly examined it and looked at Hrafn. "Defend yourself, Konungr…" he warned.

Though it was unexpected, the boy reacted immediately and lifted his sword.

Sveinn instantly charged at him, and Hrafn dodged.

Sveinn advanced further, swinging his sword again and again.

Hrafn dodged those, too, and attacked in return.

Sveinn blocked, making Hrafn retreat.

Hrafn avoided another swing and met the next one with his sword.

Sveinn smirked and increased the speed.

Hrafn followed, despite the growing tiredness.

Sveinn's eyes sparkled and he changed tactics, using twisted swings unknown to the boy.

Hrafn fought as hard as he could, dodging and twisting to avoid the blows, but Sveinn's sword touched him again and again, leaving painful bruises. His opponent looked rested and pleased with the game.

Should the sword be a real one, Hrafn would be dead long ago, but as it was wooden, he decided to stand it for as long as he could. It was a question of honor for him now. He was sure Sveinn wanted proof of his worthlessness and weakness, waiting for him to give up. So Hrafn concentrated on resisting.

At some point he felt that he would not be able to take too much more and moved back. Gathering all his strength, he lunged at Sveinn, his sword at the ready.

The latter didn't expect it, but blocked the attack, and as Hrafn was too close now, threw the boy away with a hard push of his elbow.

Hrafn received it in the chest. Blinded by the sudden pain and unable to breathe, he made a shaky step backwards and fell flat on his back. The blue sky above went dark and the boy thought he was dying. But then his lungs were filled with air again, and the darkness in front of his eyes slowly dissipated.

Sveinn stood above him.

"You win…" Hrafn groaned, thinking that he had never felt more ashamed in his life.

Sveinn smiled and held out his hand. "Nice try, Konungr. Your basics are good." Unable to tell whether it was a compliment or a mockery, Hrafn seized Sveinn's outstretched hand, and the Viking pulled him to his feet.

The boy couldn't help grimacing as his body responded with pain at that sharp movement.

Sveinn noticed it. "Sorry, my hand is heavy…"

Hrafn spotted Ari, Orm and three other Vikings who stood by the fence, watching the fight. Olaf stood near them, grinning with excitement. Hrafn scowled: was he dreaming, or was his brother happy to see him defeated so shamefully?

He mentally promised Olaf to repay in kind at the first occasion.

At that moment, Sveinn shook his hand, distracting him from his fuming thoughts. "Thanks for the fight. It was instructive."

He thrust Olaf's sword and shield into Hrafn's hands and added, "If you keep practicing like that, one day you might defeat me."

"Aye!" drawled the Vikings and Olaf together, clapping their hands.

Hrafn flashed them a dirty look.

"Never thought you would say that!" called one of the Vikings that Hrafn recognized as the red-haired lad in love with a certain Siv.

"Well, I did," calmly stated Sveinn. He easily jumped over the fence and looked back at Hrafn who stared at all of them as if they'd gone mad.

"By the way," said Sveinn, "Most of us thought you were a coward after your first order... Well, Konungr, you have proved me you're not."

With that he turned on his heels and walked away, leaving Hrafn even more puzzled.

Then Olaf ran toward him and thumped his shoulder. "Nice fight, brother!" he grinned sincerely.

Hrafn twisted his lips indignantly, "Are you mad?! I lost!"

His face blazing with excitement, Olaf shrugged. "You did. But he's the best with a sword. No one ever defeated him. You managed to stand for so long!"

Hrafn's jaw dropped. "Is he really?"

"Ari just told me. And Sveinn said you might do it one day, you heard him! Good job, brother!"

Hrafn wasn't listening. Letting the swords and the shields

fall on the grass, he hurried to the fence and climbed over it as fast as his bruised body would allow.

"I'll be back!" he threw to Olaf who raised his brows in surprise.

~~~

As if there had been no fight at all, Sveinn was flirting with a girl from a neighboring house. Charming and confident, he did it with the same ease as fighting. It looked like his plan was working: pink-faced, the girl smiled and flashed eager glances from under her lashes.

"Sveinn!" called Hrafn, arriving at full speed and making both Sveinn and the girl jump.

Sveinn turned to face him, and the boy realized that it was not the right time for an interruption.

"Er… May I have a quick word?"

"I'll be right back," Sveinn promised the girl in a low quiet voice and stepped toward Hrafn.

"Please, be quick," he whispered urgently.

"Teach me to wield the sword!" the boy blurted out.

Usually not very expressive with emotion, Sveinn raised his brows in surprise. "Well, I've never taught anyone, you know," he said. "I'm not really the teaching kind…"

"Please!" started begging Hrafn, completely forgetting that he was a king. "You are the best, and I dream of being best, too! If only I could have a couple of lessons! I promise, I'll be a very good student!"

Sveinn sighed and threw a quick glance toward the girl. "Not now," he said curtly.

"Please! I really need it!"

"I totally hate teaching…"

"Please! …"
~~~

Sveinn drew a deep breath, and then slowly blew the air out.

"All right, let's try once... I'll tell you when. Now, get lost!" he snapped.

A happy smile lit the boy's face. "Thank you! Thank you so much, Sveinn!"

Hrafn didn't feel his bruises as he ran back to tell Olaf.

"Great!" said his brother, grinning. "Will you teach me after?"

"Of course!"

Mother's tears

Together, the twins went to swim and then joined the Vikings for the evening meal.

"Hey, Olaf," whispered Hrafn halfway through their meat and cream soup. "Have you seen mother since yesterday?"

Olaf nodded, "Mmm… A couple of times. But she didn't talk to me."

"I haven't even seen her. Is she avoiding us?"

Olaf looked terrified. "You think she knows we were spying? Oh… she must be angry."

Hrafn shrugged, "I don't think she knows. At least, the rune caster didn't say he told her."

"Then what's wrong?"

"No idea. We should find her and make sure she's all right."

They hurriedly finished eating and ran home.

The house was empty. They had just missed Turid, because the fire was burning, everything was clean and tidied, their beds and clean clothes ready for them.

They made a tour around the house, but their mother was nowhere to be seen.

"Where do you think she is?" asked Olaf, worried.

"Dunno…" shrugged Hrafn. "But we need to find her!"

"All right…. You search the west side of the town, and I'll take the east. Whoever finds her brings her home."

With that they hurried in opposite directions.

Olaf ran down the paths, briefly greeting people as he passed and asking them if they had seen Turid, but he was told that she was at home, which was not very useful.

He searched the big hut that served as the kitchen for the Vikings, but with no success. He went to the sea and checked both ships, and the Viking on guard took him for Hrafn, but it was useless. Tired and hoping that his brother would be more successful, Olaf headed home, staying alert and double-checking everything on his way for any sign of his mother.

Meanwhile, Hrafn tried to do the same kind of search on the west side. Unwilling to raise any suspicions, he sought no help from others. He quickly checked the great hall—where the assemblies were held—and other buildings, but with no result.

Recalling what his mother normally did at that time, he decided that it was too late for visiting the neighbors and did not bother to ask them. Instead, he just ran down several paths, and then stopped in the crossroads, perplexed. Without his raven, searching was too difficult. In addition, he was exhausted; his whole body ached from the fight with Sveinn. Still, there was that disturbing feeling of unease for his mother. He was sure there was a problem there, and he could not leave without solving it.

Hrafn sighed and lowered himself on a big stone by the road. Rubbing his forehead with both hands, he tried to calm down and think of how his mother felt. It was unlikely she knew of their spying. So why would she avoid them? The only possible explanation seemed that the prophecy made her upset and she was trying to hide it and pull herself together alone. If that was the case, he had to find and help her, like his father would have done. The boy imagined himself in her shoes. Only last night he had been very upset, and what did he do? Instead of sleeping at home, he went wandering in the forest with his raven!

Jumping to his feet, he ran toward the forest. Night had fallen. Edging the town, the forest stood dark and mysterious, filled with animal life and rustles. But Hrafn was not afraid; he had been to the forest at night countless times with his raven. No forest spirit or troll would ever harm him.

Just like when he hunted, he carefully examined the paths until he found his mother's footprints. He followed them and got to a small clearing lit by a patch of moonlight. There on a fallen tree trunk, Turid sat, her arms tightly wrapped around her knees. She looked so lonely, sad and small that the boy felt like crying.

He moved closer and stepped on a dry branch. It made a loud crack.

Turid shivered and threw one quick glance in his direction. Fast and noiseless, she was already running away.

The boy called after her, before she would disappear. "Mother! It's me…"

She froze—a dark, slim shade between the trunks of the trees. Then she slowly turned. Hrafn could only make out her silhouette. Slowly, he stepped into the moonlight and begged, "Mother, I want to talk to you!"

Light and silent, like a spirit of the forest, she returned; the moonlight fell on her tired pale face, revealing the wet shine of her swollen eyes.

Hrafn didn't know what to say and he felt very guilty of their spying. So he just mumbled, "Mother, please, don't be angry with us. We are really sorry…"

She lowered herself on the tree trunk so that her face would be at the same level as his.

"Angry?" her whisper was somewhat shaky. "I'm not angry at either of you."

"No?" It made him feel better. "But why are you avoiding us?"

She averted her gaze. "I'm sorry, it's just… I've just been thinking of your father…" She rubbed her forehead and then looked back at the boy. "I promise, I won't be avoiding you anymore."

Her weak and tense smile made the boy frown. "It has something to do with the prophecy, hasn't it?" he asked, and her unwilling gasp indicated him that he got it right. "Mother, I know it all! We heard it! We were behind the door!"

She flinched as if he had slapped her. Her eyes widened with horror and her face went paler.

Hrafn had never felt so badly in his life. "Mother, I'm so sorry! It was my idea. We wanted so much to know the future, in case it would be about us."

Turid said nothing. She stared at her knees and bitter tears ran down her cheeks.

The boy fell on his knees and gripped her hand with both of his. "Please, mother, don't cry! … We are sorry! We won't ever do it again, I promise! Mother… you cannot be so upset because of our spying!"

She looked at him and shook her head, her hand ruffling his hair. He felt so relieved that he sighed.

Turid wiped her cheeks with her hands and looked heavenward. She was struggling to stop the tears.

The boy remained silent, gathering his thoughts. He had to deal with it now. With all of it.

"If it's not our spying, it must be the prophecy itself that upsets you, no? Mother, look at me…"

She met his serious gaze, and he went on. "I know my destiny doesn't seem very promising, but it can hardly be changed."

All the woman's efforts to stop the tears failed. She had to press her fist to her mouth so that not to sob.

"Remember, father had always told us that because everyone will die sooner or later, we have to enjoy every moment of our life like the last one. Remember?"

She nodded, her shoulders slightly shaking.

"Right now I'm alive, safe and healthy. So forget that prophecy and please don't cry."

Sobbing, she nodded again.

Hrafn stood and held his arms toward her. She hugged him hurriedly and sat him on her knees, pressing him against her, as if someone was about to take him from her. The boy didn't object; after all, no one was around to see them.

"I love you," she whispered.

"I love you too," came his muffled voice. "We still have a lot of time to spend together… and I have a war to win." He looked up at her. "We need you here and now. As for the future, it will just come when it has to. Agreed?"

"Agreed…" she whispered and hugged him again, kissing the top of his head.

They sat still for some time. Turid made a huge effort to suffocate the crying. When finally it seemed she had succeeded, she broke the silence. "You know, I was right naming you the king," she said.

"Why? Did the rune caster really tell you I'll win the war?" Hrafn asked. "We didn't hear that one."

"Hmmm… He must have known you were there, for he whispered that in my ear right before I left."

The boy thoughtfully scratched the tip of his nose. "I do not know how I'm supposed to do it."

His mother shrugged. "I am terribly sorry, but I don't know how I can help you here." She heaved a sigh. "I know, I should have done it myself, but the truth is… that I'm just scared!" There was so much disgust in her voice that Hrafn tightened his hug, pressing himself to her.

"It's all right being afraid," he said calmly. "After all, men are supposed to be better warriors than women, and as I've been learning the war craft, I may come up with a plan. You said the rune caster saw me doing it."

Turid's expression was still torn. He put both his palms on her wet cheeks and forced her to meet his gaze. "Look, I really don't blame you for choosing me. Taking father's place is an honor. But we've been so sure it was going to be Olaf that it sort of... that it… oh! I just still can't believe it!"

She gave him a weak smile. "Me too, I'm still having trouble to believe it all." Her gaze turned grave. "Listen, no matter what, you can always count on me. I'll help you as much as I can, I'll always be with you and I'll willingly die for you, just like for your brother!"

Hrafn's eyes widened with horror. "Don't you even think of dying for me! When I die, you must live! Life is wonderful and we have to enjoy it as much as we can! Anyway, afterwards we'll all meet in Valhalla. And there is Olaf for you to take care of, and then there is going to be his children and grandchildren!"

At those words, Turid began weeping again.

Hrafn patiently hugged her and gently patted her back, "Cry it out, mother, you'll feel better."

She found it very strange to hear from him her own words, but deep inside she knew she needed to be told that—she needed to let it all out. So she abandoned herself to her emotions, burying her swollen face in Hrafn's hair and weeping so hard that her body shook, weeping for all the pain of the last couple of days and back to the moment when she said her last good-bye to her husband before he sailed away to meet his death.

In her lap, Hrafn sat very still, gently stroking her back. And she clung to him, like she used to cling to her mother, then to her husband, craving understanding and comfort.

She wept for what seemed her too long, but when it finally passed, she felt blissful relief and sincere gratitude toward her little man.

Hrafn raised his head to look at her. His back was sore and aching, but nothing in the world would ever make him confess it. Perceiving the positive change of her mood, he sought to busy her mind with some action. "Can you advise me about the coming war?"

Watching her face, he noticed with joy the results of his comforting—she was no longer upset, but thinking of the future with calm and determination.

"My advice would be the following," she said finally, "stay calm and do not let the panic seize you."

Hrafn nodded, "Thanks, I'll remember that. Just promise me not to worry."

A faint smile pulled the corners of her mouth. "You know, that'll be too hard…"

"At least, promise me to try!"

"Aye. I promise."

"Good," he whispered, hugging her again.

She caressed his golden hair.

"Oh, mother, Olaf is waiting for us," suddenly remembered Hrafn. "Let's go home."

They walked home hand in hand, in peace and harmony.

~~~

Olaf waited by the fire. As the door opened, he jumped to his feet.
~~~

"Mother! We've been looking for you everywhere!"

Turid hugged him with tenderness. "I'm sorry. I was just feeling too upset."

"It's the prophecy," Hrafn explained. "But we dealt with that."

"Good," grinned Olaf. "There is nothing to be upset about. You know, Hrafn decided to sail the day after tomorrow. And guess what? I am ruling with him!"

A blazing smile lit Turid's face. "I'm glad to hear that," she said. "I think you'd better stay together."

The twins grinned mischievously and exchanged looks.

"Sure," said Olaf. "Did we ever thank you for making us twins?"

The Preparations

The next morning, Olaf and Hrafn were up at the dawn.

The Vikings met them by the ships, impatient to do something. For the first time, the boys would participate in the preparation of a war trip.

Ari kindly helped, explaining things every now and then. The Vikings knew well what had to be done, so orders were unnecessary, and the boys fetched and carried small things. At midday, when everybody ate and rested, Örjan arrived.

"Hrafn, I'd like to have a word," he said shyly.

Still chewing his food, Hrafn stood up and left the table.

Together they walked to the sea, beyond the earshot of the others.

Örjan was nervous. Hrafn knew that particularity of his, so he began speaking first. "Uncle, I wanted to tell you that my kingship doesn't change a thing; you remain a good friend of mine and once the war is over, I'll certainly come to help you with your crops."

Örjan grinned, "Thank you, Hrafn... I wanted to talk to you about the war."

"Of course. What's that?"

The giant averted his glance, his fingers fumbling with a lacing of his shirt.

"It's... I... I want to go fight with you. Take me to your army! Torgeir was my brother and I feel I have to do something to avenge his death!" He looked at his nephew, not really sure he said it right, but not knowing what else to say.

The boy didn't pause to think. "Of course," he agreed. "I'll be very happy to have you by my side!"

Örjan beamed, relieved, and added, "I promise I won't question orders!"

Hrafn's voice was thick with emotions "Thank you."

Örjan had no idea how relieved Hrafn felt to have someone perfectly reliable, someone who would support him without questioning his decisions, no matter what they would be.

~~~

After the meal, the twins spent some time at home, discussing their plans. Hrafn explained to Olaf that the raven flew forward to scout the Foreign mainland and find out something about the enemy plans, but that he hadn't reached them yet.

Olaf agreed that it was a clever move even though, unlike Hrafn, he didn't think that the Foreigners would attack their town just yet.

"Why would they do that? If I were their king, I would have won back the fortress first and then I would have made other plans."

Hrafn shrugged.

"It is possible. But we are outnumbered. We have to consider all the possibilities. The fortress is the first point that we conquered on their lands. If they are cunning, they will let us believe in our possible victory and wait until we move all of our warriors there. Meanwhile, they will attack
~~~

our unprotected lands and then get back and finish off all those who are in the fortress."

Olaf waved his hand. "That sounds too far fetched."

"No, it doesn't."

"Yes it does! You need every single warrior you can get, especially because we are outnumbered! Sometimes a dozen more warriors can swing the outcome of the war!"

Hrafn sighed. "Good, you are right. But anyway, we can't leave the town unprotected. Because you never know who else would like to take advantage of it and conquer our lands!"

Olaf couldn't object to this. "So, how many people will stay here?" he asked.

Hrafn shrugged. "I don't know yet. The warriors can disagree with this plan."

Olaf scratched his head and thought for a while. "You know what I think?" he said finally and bent toward his brother, lowering his voice. "You are the only one who can win because of the bird. No one else has that. So your raven is our main asset!"

Hrafn thoughtfully watched his brother. "That makes sense," he finally said. "The rune caster told me to use 'my particular strength.' "

Olaf nodded, his eyes shining with excitement.

"Olaf, you are the only one to know it, apart from the rune caster, but he doesn't count. In this case, you'd better stay here, in the town, so I will be able to warn you of anything through the raven."

Olaf moaned with disappointment. But Hrafn went on, without giving him the time to interrupt.

"The raven hasn't reached the Foreign land yet and we know nothing about their plans, but if I delay our departure longer, the Vikings will make a mutiny. I will leave and you will take my place here and organize the protection and the defense of the town if the need should arise."

Olaf didn't want to stay. He had always dreamed of sailing to a war, and now, when his dream was finally about to come true, he was being denied it! The prospect of being in charge of the town was pale in comparison to a war trip. What if no defense was needed?

Hrafn knew how his brother felt. They could share feelings sometimes. At the same time, it was important to protect the town, and Olaf's presence would leave a possibility of communication between them.

Olaf heaved a sigh. He knew Hrafn had a point. In addition, he still felt ashamed of his childish reaction when his brother was named konungr—Hrafn had never shown or felt any jealousy when they were sure it would be him, Olaf. Hrafn was happy for him and proud and supportive, while he ... Olaf felt bad for his behavior and wanted to make amends for it.

"All right, let's do it that way." he agreed, unable to hide his disappointment. He would sail later.

~~~

Soon after that, Hrafn started naming people for the crew of each ship.

They had in their possession two large warships and one small. The twins decided that the small one was to stay, which did not really please some Vikings. Hrafn would sail on one of the large ships, and Orm and Kirk would be in his crew together with his uncle Örjan. He wanted Ari to command the second ship.
~~~

"Why are you taking Kirk with you?" whispered Olaf. "Put him with Ari."

Hrafn shook his head. "He is the most upset with everything I do or say, I'd better keep people like that close."

Olaf rolled his eyes. "It's crazy! If you keep them all on your ship, you are sure to have a mutiny, or worse—to get killed before you even reach the Foreigners!"

Hrafn turned to look at his brother. Olaf was right. "We'll divide them then?"

Olaf nodded, his expression serious. "Yes. Make sure you separate each of them from his best friend. It will weaken the opposition."

It was easier to say then to do. They didn't know the names of some of the warriors, let alone the connections between them.

Finally, Hrafn called Ari and asked his advice. The latter was happy to offer his help and his intervention visibly reassured some warriors who clearly doubted Hrafn's abilities to command.

"Thanks for your trust, Konungr." Ari said. "As I am not on the same ship with you, take Sveinn to your crew. He is very good on the rudder and he knows how to read the stars and the sky just as well as Kirk does."

Hrafn eagerly followed this advice—he itched to have his sword-wielding lesson with Sveinn and thus Sveinn's presence on his ship had a double advantage.

Ari was really helpful—he called each warrior by his name and mentioned the biggest strengths or weaknesses of each. Hrafn knew he was doing it on purpose, but he did it naturally, without stressing Hrafn's ignorance or making it look like a lesson. Both Olaf and Hrafn learned a lot and felt very grateful to Ari.

Each warship was to carry sixty warriors. The rest—two

dozen men—would stay in the town under Olaf's command. The fact that another child was given command only worsened the situation. But angry protests quickly turned into low muttering because someone spotted the rune caster walking by and the old man waved his hand in a general greeting. The rune caster was deeply respected, not because people feared him, but because almost everyone had used his prophecies and seen them turn into life; no one had a reason to accuse him of lying.

"Why aren't they sailing with us?" asked someone with glaring disappointment, waving his hand toward the group of those who were staying. Several other Vikings muttered in agreement.

Hrafn turned to him and explained, "We can't leave the town with no protection at all, can we? It's a war, after all."

"Sure," Kirk cut across indignantly. "But it's unnecessary to have that many people here when they are much more needed on board! Who will attack us, anyway? All the neighbors are our vassals or allies! To prove it, you have some of their people right here, in your crew!"

Hrafn listened and after some consideration, he announced, "Maybe you're right… Let's see…" he turned to face the Vikings that were selected to stay. "You and you," he called, pointing his finger at the two men who seemed most unhappy with their staying. "One of you joins my ship and the other goes with Ari."

Somewhat mollified, the warriors followed. Hrafn turned back to Olaf, recalling what they had been talking about.

Kirk's face went bright red; that puppy was mocking him! Burning fury washed over him. His fists clenched and a snarl started building in his chest. His strongest urge was to throw the boy across the knee and to spank him until he fully understood the idea of "respect one's elders"!

But he didn't make a move—Hrafn's uncle, who had just appeared out of nowhere as the boy's bodyguard, made a step toward him. Örjan didn't make a sound, but his frown was loaded with threat. Despite Örjan being a farmer, he knew how to wield an axe and the impressive size of his fists indicated that he was a formidable opponent in a hand to hand fight. Kirk decided to postpone his educational session. He lowered his fists, but the suppressed fury raged inside him, only getting stronger because he was denied to let it out.

Watching him, Olaf silently laughed. "I wish I could go with you just to be able to look at Kirk's face when he reacts at your orders!" he whispered.

Hrafn half-smiled, his eyes serious. "Well, I'm not exactly in the position to find it funny," he complained. "I wish you were going with me, but apart from you, no one can help me here."

Olaf grudgingly nodded, "I guess, next time."

~~~

By sunset the ships were ready to sail.

Before dinner, Hrafn gathered all the Vikings who were leaving, as well as those who were staying. He told them, "We should have a system of signs to communicate between us in case we need to act in silence."

"We do have some," interrupted him Ari. "The open palm means 'wait'. When you beckon with the right arm, it means 'attack'. The same with the left arm means 'follow'. Otherwise, every captain knows what to do."

"Right…" the boy mused. "It's just that I think we should act more like a team. What if it gives better results? Wouldn't it be easier if everyone knew what the others were doing?"
~~~

The Vikings remained silent, but their expressions indicated that Hrafn still had their full attention. He went on. "I suggest we come up with signs for 'row', 'stop rowing', 'hoist the sail', 'lower the sail', 'weigh the anchor', 'throw the anchor', 'fire arrows', 'stand by the rail'…"All of those had been invented by Olaf and himself long ago. It was their secret system in their games, and, knowing the efficiency of it, the boy wanted to test it in real life.

The Vikings didn't seem particularly excited about it. Nonetheless, they repeated the signs after Hrafn several times with rather bored expressions, and then hurried to the table.

I Am Sailing!

At night, Hrafn couldn't sleep. The coming war trip occupied his thoughts, making him restless with expectation and anxiety.

To his relief, Olaf couldn't sleep either. Together they crept out of the house, trying not to wake their mother, and sat in the yard until the dawn, discussing again and again their plans and different turns the war might take. Hrafn had not left yet, but they were already missing each other, and somehow going through all the details together for a thousand and third time made them feel better.

Turid woke before the dawn and insisted they eat together. But they ate in silence, each of them lost in thoughts of the upcoming events.

Before they left the house, Turid spoke, "Olaf, Hrafn, there is something I want to tell you before you go."

The twins both feared a long, sentimental farewell ceremony that would make them feel uncomfortable. Yet they could not dare deny their mother such a small thing.

Turid said in a calm and even voice, "First, I want you to know that I completely trust all your plans, whatever they might be. I am sure, both of you know how to do it the best way possible. However, I am a woman, and most importantly, your mother. I want to give you something for gods' protection, just to keep myself from too much worry."

She removed from around her neck two leather thongs with small stones hanging on them. Each stone had a different runic sign engraved on it.

She knelt before Hrafn and slipped one thong around his neck. Then she kissed his forehead and both cheeks. She repeated the same procedure with Olaf.

"Please, keep them with you all the time, and may gods protect both of you!" she said quietly and her voice quavered. "I love both of you very much."

~~~

All the farewells over, the two ships left the docks and glided proudly toward the rising sun, under the admiring gaze of the crowd.

The morning was beautiful and fresh, and back in the sea, the Vikings felt cheerful, rowing energetically and talking.

As they left the bay, the strong fair wind caught the ships; the sailors piled their oars and put up their yellow and red sails.

Hrafn savored every moment; it was his first big sailing and everything was exciting and new. He wanted to try and row a little, but with the strong wind propelling them, there was no need.

Some Vikings slept; others talked, played with tiny wooden figures that they moved across a checked wooden board, or honed their weapons.

Hrafn sat by the rudder, watching the sea and the quickly retreating land. It all still seemed unbelievable; only a week ago he played with Olaf on their tiny boat, unaware that soon he would be sailing a warship as a konungr.

Orm came and sat down next to him. "You seem thoughtful, Konungr," he said.
~~~

Hrafn met his gaze and shrugged. "I still can't believe it all," he confessed. "I'm living a dream."

The old Viking chuckled. "The war is not exactly a dream, but rather a nightmare. Killing for the sake of killing is not good at all."

His gaze lost somewhere in the waves, the boy nodded. "I know. But shouldn't we just enjoy the present moment as it is, instead of imagining all sorts of bad stuff?"

"Sounds so much like your father!"

The boy grinned. He liked being compared to his father. Then he looked eagerly at Orm. "Can you please tell me some legends?" he asked.

Orm's gray mustache went up and wrinkles around his eyes got deeper as he smiled. "Why not? Let me tell you about the so called Star Gate…"

~~~

At the evening, Sveinn decided to give Hrafn his sword-wielding lesson.

"You must pay close mind," he informed the boy, who burned with excitement. "The swords are real this time, and you don't want to break them before the battle."

For the first time, the boy took his father's sword. It was a long, heavy sword with a single-handed hilt and a lobed pommel. The blade was straight, double-edged, with a deep fuller running its length. It was pattern welded and thus a flame-like mysterious pattern decorated its entire surface.

Sveinn instantly recognized the sword and his lips curved in a crooked smile. "No offense, but it might be too heavy for you."

Hrafn shrugged. "I don't have another."
~~~

Both of them took their shields and went to the center of the ship, which was the widest.

They tried several basics that the boy already knew, but he did not object, for he had promised to be a good student. He badly wanted Sveinn to teach him and tried hard to satisfy his new teacher.

His father's sword was too heavy for him indeed. Soon his arm grew tired, but he kept fighting, clenching his teeth.

"Turn your shield outward a little," corrected Sveinn. "You need your enemy's sword not to break it, but to slide on it as far from you as possible, because it will give you a little time. Let's try again!"

Sveinn didn't go farther than the basics, showing him tiny details that he never thought of before.

"Faster on that one!"

"I just did it a moment ago! You have to pay mind, to remember it and to be ready for it as it comes for the second time!"

"Here, as you jump over the sword, watch your arms: it's your opportunity to attack by surprise!"

"Always stay alert! You must control every muscle of your body at the same time, and the sword must be part of you!"

Hrafn listened, but was so exhausted that he thought his knees would buckle. Meanwhile Sveinn looked calm and energetic as always. He mercilessly made the boy repeat the jumps and the moves again and again.

When he finally announced that the lesson—or rather the torture—was over, Hrafn couldn't believe his ears.

Heavily panting, his hands on the hips, the boy swallowed and asked in a half-whisper, "Will you give me another lesson?"

Sveinn shot him a brief glance and examined his own sword, his expression unfathomable. Then he carefully put it into the scabbard and announced. "All right. I will give you another one. I'm not telling you when, but make sure you have learned all of this by that time."

"I will," said Hrafn, thinking that he would need months to master it all. "Thank you."

Sveinn's eyes sparkled and a slight smirk touched his lips. "You are welcome."

Hrafn dragged himself to an empty corner and, before he knew, fell fast asleep.

When he woke at dawn, his first thought was to practice his lesson.

The rhythm of life on the ship was different from the one on the dry land—Vikings took turns to sleep, and half of the crew was always awake, making it impossible to practice unnoticed. The boy felt really annoyed with that, especially given that he had never practiced on his own before. Plus, the crew was not particularly fond of him, and thus much more willing to mock his mistakes. But the need to be as ready as possible for his next lesson was much stronger; he had no choice but to clench his teeth and do it under the curious stares of the Vikings.

They observed him with interest, and very fortunately, no one made a single comment nor laughed. Soon Hrafn became so focused that he forgot everything else but his sword and shield. Since yesterday, his muscles felt very sore and out of control, and it demanded him all of his willpower and nerve to push himself forward and to keep working. But the more he warmed up, the less his muscles ached, and before he knew it, he had spent quite a while practicing.

Orm interrupted him, announcing that the morning meal was ready. Hrafn carefully put his father's sword into the scabbard and after a quick wash, joined the others.

The weather was held good and the wind remained strong and fair. Obviously awaiting Hrafn's reaction, Kirk stated loudly, "If the weather is just as good, we will be there sooner! Three days, I'd say!"

The boy shrugged impassively. "Good."

The day went just like the previous one. For exercise, the Vikings rowed for some time, competing between the two ships, but then the midday heat made them stop and rest.

Hrafn seized the opportunity and tried to row with the others. The oar was nearly twenty feet long and the task was not an easy one. With his muscles sore from the sword practice, it was even worse. He could only stand some thirty strokes, but felt satisfied that he had tried.

Later at the evening, the boy tried to practice again, but he was too tired and had to abandon it very soon. Sveinn saw him doing it, but didn't show any reaction.

At dinner, Hrafn sat next to Sveinn, intrigued by this dark-haired Viking who seemed so much in control of his emotions. He wanted to talk to him.

Sveinn just threw him a quick glance and moved, making space for him.

It turned out that Hrafn was not the only one interested in Sveinn's experiences—the young red-haired lad sat across from them. Hrafn learned that his name was Knut. Knut admired Sveinn's undeniable success with women and hoped to learn something from him.

As for Sveinn, he was not intending to talk at all, giving the food his full attention, determined to enjoy every bit of it. But if Hrafn was politely waiting for him to finish, Knut was more direct and impatient.

"Hey, Sveinn," he called. "So, what about your Eydis? Did you sleep with her just for fun, or are you really planning to come back to her?" Knut meant no offense. It was just in his nature: his stare was innocently curious and sincere.

Sveinn took his time finishing chewing, and then commented in an offhand tone, "If you are trying to impress a woman, which is what really interests you, being that bold and direct will only ruin your effort."

Knut's blue eyes widened. "But… but how do you want me to talk, then?" he asked, confused.

"Delicately," Sveinn said, putting a slice of cheese on his bread.

Ottar, who sat next to Knut, elbowed him and laughed. "You are wasting your time, lad. Where did you see a delicate warrior? He sees you're hooked and is playing on your ignorance to laugh after!"

Sveinn chuckled. "Sure! Listen to Ottar! He never seduced anyone but Asta, who knew him ever since he was born. As there is still no other woman, he will end up marrying her."

Everyone laughed.

Ottar looked pissed off. "No, I won't!" he retorted. "Watch out, Sveinn, or I'll marry your Eydis just in revenge!"

Sveinn just shrugged. "Go ahead, if you want. But I seriously doubt it."

Knut's eyes shone again. He held his hand palm forward, interrupting Ottar who wanted to say something else, and exclaimed. "Come on, Sveinn. Tell me what's the secret!"

Calm and undisturbed as usual, Sveinn met his gaze. "There is no secret. It's like fighting: watch, listen, pay attention and try to anticipate—"

"Yes, of course!" cut across him another Viking. "Hide behind your shield, jump at her unexpected and always, always attack!"

A thunder of laughter shook the ship.

A mysterious smile played on Sveinn's lips while Knut

was completely confused. He kept turning his head from one side to another, blinking in bewilderment.

Ottar patted his back. "C'mon, lad. Stop dreaming. Sveinn will never reveal his secrets. He is a son of a blacksmith…"

This time, Hrafn's jaw dropped. "Really?" he asked with the same admiring expression that Knut wore just a moment ago.

Sveinn gave him a quick glance and took a bite of his bread. Then he nodded.

This time Hrafn's curiosity was stronger than his sense of good manners. To prevent any possible intervention and change of subject, he hurried to ask, "So you can make swords as well?"

Sveinn took his time to swallow the food and answered, "I know how to do it, if that's what you mean. But as you can see, I chose to be a Viking."

"A big loss for our people, I will always say so!" commented Orm, appearing out of nowhere. He sat next to Hrafn and explained, "Not that he is a bad warrior, but his father was from Arabia, and knew the secret of making fine swords."

His eyes wide with admiration, the boy looked back at Sveinn.

"Is your father still alive?" he asked.

Sveinn shook his head. "He died by accident about eight winters ago."

"Do you have any other family left?"

"Certainly, somewhere in the south."

"Are you intending to find them one day?"

Sveinn gave him a thoughtful glance. "I've never been there in my life. I was born in our town and my father had never traveled again, as far as I remember."

"He must have told you a lot of interesting stories about his country!" marveled the boy.

This time Sveinn didn't answer, staring at his loaf of bread.

Hrafn vividly imagined his own father, when he was teaching or telling stories. A devastating feeling of emptiness swept over him and he felt a lump form in his throat. Swallowing to dislodge it, he hurried to apologize.

"I'm sorry, you must miss him…" He made his hoarse voice very low, so that only Sveinn would hear.

Sveinn gave him a long glance, his brows raised. His arms wrapped around his knees, the boy stared unseeingly at the deck, deep in his thoughts. It occurred to Sveinn that Hrafn must have a hard time coping with it all. For the first time, he felt empathy for the new konungr.

A Prophetic Dream

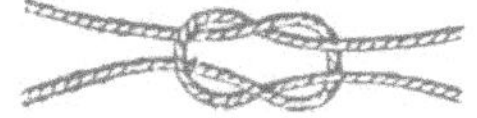

Hrafn woke in a jolt. His raven had called to him.

The sun hadn't risen, but the sky was turning gray, the wind falling slightly. Next to the boy, his uncle Örjan snored in his sleep.

Trying to shake off the rest of his sleep, the boy jumped to his feet and leaned on the wooden rail. He closed his eyes and took a deep breath. In a matter of a heartbeat he was in the head of his raven, looking through the bird's eyes. He was soaring very high in the morning sky and strong, fresh wind pleasantly stroked his feathers. Flying was good, a great pleasure, and the boy marveled at it just as much as his bird. Far below, seven ships glided on the waves, their sails bulging with the wind. From the height of his flight, they looked small like toys. They were large warships. Foreigners' warships. Raven's sight was so sharp that Hrafn could clearly distinguish the cargo—stones and weapons of all sorts, and the mail hauberks of the crew.

Sharing thoughts was so much quicker than exchanging words. In the time of one breath, the boy knew that the bird had reached the Foreign mainland and found that their warships were gone. It took the raven the whole night to find them and discover their plans.

"They are heading for the town," the bird silently informed him. *"They have nearly one day on you. Hurry."*

Hrafn's eyes flew wide open, his heart thumping. The town had no chance against such an army. He had guessed right the Foreigners' plans, but it didn't make him feel any better. He spun around and called, "We are turning back! Now!"

"What?!" gasped Ottar, who sat nearby.

Hrafn turned to Sveinn, who was on the rudder.

"Sveinn, turn us back, quickly!"

This time, Sveinn didn't bother to hide his bewilderment. "Konungr, what's the matter with you? We are more than halfway to the fortress!"

"Turn the ship, please! I'll explain later!" Hrafn put two fingers in his mouth and whistled. The sharp sound covered the wind and the waves, making most of the Vikings jump. Even on the second ship people heard it. Hrafn shouted, "Start wearing! We are going back!"

He instantly ordered the same thing to the second ship through the sign system he had taught them.

To say that the Vikings were flabbergasted was an understatement. Instead of following the orders, the warriors scowled and shouted.

"We are almost there!"

"Are you mad?"

"We can't turn back!"

"Vikings are not cowards!"

"Are you scared or what?"

"Told you he wouldn't have the nerve!"

The last one belonged to Kirk. Arms crossed over his chest, the boy returned them their scowl.

"I am the konungr here, and I just gave orders" he said, boiling inside.

His red hair messy after sleep, Örjan made his way to his nephew. He didn't say a word, but decisively stood by

Hrafn's side, thus making his opinion more than clear.

Hrafn realized but too well the urgency of the matter. But no one around him was even thinking of obeying. The angry, agitated Vikings around him left him frustrated, not knowing what to do.

Meanwhile, the arguing was growing louder and angrier.

"What about our people in the fortress? We cannot abandon them!"

"Running away is a shame!"

"We want to fight!"

"Listen!" yelled Hrafn. "You'll get your fight sooner than you have expected!"

But no one seemed to hear him. Anger burned him from inside. Their time was short and there he was, unable to make them do what was needed! He knew all along that it had to be expected, but the helplessness of his position was driving him mad.

Suddenly Sveinn whistled, just like Hrafn did a moment ago. Everyone fell silent, staring at him.

"We are losing our time arguing," he said, annoyed, and turned toward Hrafn. "Konungr, if you want us to follow you, you have to explain. We are people just like you, and we need to understand. So tell us, why do we need to go back?"

Hrafn felt like crying. Sveinn was right while his anger had cost them so much precious time! Hrafn was used to Olaf's instant understanding and following that it didn't occur to him on the spot that the Vikings would not obey. Of course, he could not tell them everything. Drawing a deep breath, he said, "The Foreigners are about to attack our town."

For a couple of heartbeats, everyone remained silent, digesting the information. Then Kirk asked skeptically, "How do you know that?"

Hrafn was ready. He had been expecting this question ever since his first order. He looked Kirk in the eye and stated, "A prophetic dream."

Now everyone around him shook their heads. Prophetic dreams were not unheard of—various sagas and legends mentioned them, and most believed in their existence. But none of the warriors had seen their war plans based upon one.

Finally, Knut broke the silence.

"But how can you be sure? I mean… it could be just a nightmare or something!"

Hrafn's whole being screamed for action. "I am absolutely sure! I've had it before! I swear by all the gods! You can cut me into pieces if I'm wrong! Foreigner ships have one whole day on us!"

"But what if they don't intend to attack the town?" asked Ottar.

Hrafn looked heavenward. "Then we'll take advantage and crush their ships! Come on, let's hurry! We have to stop them before it's too late!"

Perplexed rather than convinced, the Vikings finally began moving.

"We left so many warriors in the town! Can't they protect it?" muttered Kirk as he passed.

Hrafn flashed him a disdainful look. "You really think they are enough to stand against seven full Foreigner boats?"

Kirk couldn't object to that one. Scowling at the boy, he muttered, "If all of this is rubbish…"

He didn't finish his threat, but at the moment Hrafn couldn't care less.

Meanwhile, Ottar swam to the second ship and explained the situation. Hrafn never knew what his arguments were, or what their reaction was, but Ari obeyed, which was all that mattered. Both ships turned and headed back, their bows cutting through the blue spines of the waves.

The wind remained strong for the whole day, and their advance was steady. By evening, when Hrafn and half of the Vikings were at their meal, a big black raven appeared in the darkening sky. He soared over the ship and then flew down in circles, before landing at Hrafn's outstretched arm.

Knut, who was seated nearby, lifted his red-haired head and spotted the bird.

"A raven!" he exclaimed. "That's a bad omen!"

"He's mine," the boy reassured him, his full attention turned to the bird.

He made some space on the deck next to him and carefully spread all of his food there. When the raven ate its fill, Hrafn held his cup to it, letting the bird drink some water under the Vikings' surprised glances.

"Isn't that too much care for a pet?" asked someone, but Hrafn didn't react. No matter how much he wanted to earn the respect of the Vikings, he would have never confessed them that it was only thanks to his raven that he knew about the Foreigners' attack.

Then, while the raven was resting, Hrafn retrieved a wide leather strap from one of his boots and scratched on it with his knife, "Attack: 7 ships". Making sure it was clearly seen and well-engraved, he bent down and carefully tied the strap around the bird's left leg. The raven waited, not moving. Only its beetle-like eyes scrutinized the ship and the people around.

When Hrafn finished, he held his arm for the raven to hop on it, and slowly stood. The raven took off and in several powerful flaps of wings rose high into the dark sky. The boy watched the bird until it disappeared. Sveinn's calm voice pulled him out of his thoughts.

"Nice plan, Konungr. You can really make the raven deliver your messages?"

Hrafn shrugged. "I hope so. We are late and I can only try to warn them so that they get ready."

~~~

They sailed the next day and most of the night. At the dawn, they finally reached the fjord. Stopping behind the rocks at the entrance of the bay where they could not be seen from the land, the Vikings joined the bows of the ships so that Hrafn could go to Ari's ship for a quick word.

They didn't talk for long. Ari lit two oil lamps and handed one to Hrafn before the boy went back to his ship.

"Lower the sail," he ordered. "Best archers, gather in the middle and light your arrows, others get back to the oars, but keep your weapons ready. Let's move while I explain our tactics…"

The oars rhythmically cut into the water and Hrafn's ship entered the bay, closely followed by Ari's.
~~~

The Battle

Though Hrafn told the others what was happening, none were keen to believe it, and some of them, including Kirk, seriously doubted it. But the sight the bay offered took all of them by surprise.

Seven of the largest and finest Foreign ships advanced on the town in a wedge formation, firing arrows and stones simultaneously, and making it difficult for the town's people to respond. From their position, the Vikings could not see what was happening in the town, and loud war cries of the Foreigners echoed around, making it impossible to distinguish any other sound.

Hrafn was anxious, about to enter his first real battle and felt ice in the pit of his stomach. Their plan had been thought over very carefully, yet the difference in numbers between the foes was great. The enemy was even more terrifying up close. All of his senses much more alive than ever before, Hrafn knew exactly what was happening in the town, thanks to his raven. Observing the scene from two different views at the same time was making chaos in his head. He struggled to keep them separate.

Hrafn's ship quickly headed toward the last ship on the left, while Ari's was attacking the last ship on the right.

"Now!" Sveinn quietly ordered when they were close enough.

The Vikings shot simultaneously. The air whistled as over a hundred flaming arrows rose high, like a flight of lethal bees, and carried by the fair wind, fell over the Foreign ships.

The Foreigners yelled in pain and fear, spotting the Vikings behind them.

"Don't stop! Burn them!" shouted Hrafn, loosening another burning arrow. The oarsmen stopped rowing and joined the archers. They didn't need to advance further. They had to draw the Foreign ships out of the battle.

The fair wind acted as their ally, spreading the fire. But it was just the beginning. The second to last Foreign ships quickly turned and joined the battle. Their arrows and spears fell on both Viking ships, too.

The Vikings were expecting it—half of the crew instantly focused on the new enemy, replying with fire arrows. They had to be quick. It was their only chance to win. They shoot arrows as fast as they could, aiming for the ship parts as much as for the people. When there were no more arrows left, stones and spears replaced them.

So far, the plan was working: the two last ships of the wedge were badly burning.

The fire was spreading on the second to last ships, too. Panic-stricken, the Foreigners struggled in vain to extinguish it. Even though they were partially succeeding, it was clear that with so much wind sooner or later their efforts would be doomed. Nonetheless they kept fighting, and the Vikings had to form a shield wall to protect themselves.

The warning came from the raven—the Foreign ships that formed the top of the wedge changed their tactics, too. Two of them were now heading toward Ari. If the burning ship that Ari's crew was fighting would join them and turn, Ari's ship would be doomed.

"They don't see it," the bird explained, *"it's a trap."*

Hrafn glanced around. He didn't know what to do.

"Watch out!" Sveinn pulled him away just in time to avoid a deadly spear. It scratched the boy's arm, tearing the fabric of his sleeve.

Hrafn's mind didn't really register it yet.

"Ari's in trouble," he blurted out. "The Foreigners want to trap them between two ships."

Sveinn heard. His shield at the ready, he stood up and looked around.

Hrafn threw another stone.

"Can we help them?" he asked.

Sveinn crouched, stopping an arrow with his shield.

"We can try and pass in the middle. With a little luck, we'll get the burning ship out of the way."

Hrafn glanced at the two ships that were separating them from the front of the bay.

"Aren't they too close?"

Sveinn was already moving toward the rudder.

"Ari won't stand three ships at once. We have to try."

Hrafn nodded, "Do it."

"All to the oars! Shields!" Sveinn yelled.

Hrafn couldn't help admiring his crew—they were quick to react and their moves were precise.

The Foreigners instantly understood that Hrafn's ship was trying to pass in the middle, between the already burning second to last ships of the wedge. They were brave warriors and they jumped on the opportunity. They abandoned their attempts to stop the fire and seized their oars, determined to crash Hrafn's ship at any price.

Leaving Sveinn on the rudder, Hrafn climbed on the mast. He needed to try to signal the town. He quickly climbed to the very top. Seizing it with both legs, he lifted both arms in the air, first making a circle and then a right angle. He repeated the signs three times, but could not tell whether anyone saw it, because he was distracted by the quickly approaching burning ships.

Sveinn hastened the rhythm and the oarsmen worked hard, propelling the ship toward the enemy at full speed. Their ships burning, the Foreigners bravely plied their oars, rushing toward the Vikings from both sides. Their ships were heavier and slower, but they spared no effort. They were close, too close.

Hrafn felt his whole body tense like a drawn bow. Every buffet of the wind enveloped him with smoke and ash. From where he was, getting through looked impossible.

"Sveinn, are you sure?" he called.

"Trust me," was the answer.

For what seemed an eternity, they advanced at full speed toward the yelling Foreigners.

"We are doomed!" flashed in Hrafn's mind as their bow entered the space between the two advancing ships.

"At three pull up the oars!" commanded Sveinn, his voice firm with concentration. The oarsmen kept their rhythm, rowing with all their might. "One… Two…"

Hrafn bit his fist so that not to yell—one of the Foreign ships was almost on their port side!

"Three!"

All the oars rose toward the center of the ship, like claws hidden in the paw of a cat, freeing the space between them and the Foreigners. The Viking ship kept advancing with Sveinn carefully maneuvering the rudder.

That sudden move surprised the Foreigners: several exclamations broke out of their unanimous war cries, but it didn't stop them.

In front of them, tense and silent, the Vikings froze with their oars, staring at the approaching ships.

Ten feet… seven… three… the Foreigners' bow was now so close to their stern that Sveinn could have touched it with an outstretched arm. Hrafn stopped breathing. Yet Sveinn looked undisturbed.

The oars rose again to propel the Foreigners farther forward. Hrafn would have screamed, but his voice was no longer available.

The bow of the burning ship was approaching, fast and unstoppable, ready to crash its prey. Less than an arm's length! Foreigners yelled triumphantly and Hrafn was ready to die. Suddenly Sveinn pulled on the rudder. Their ship jerked to the right and Hrafn nearly fell from the mast.

But it was enough. They avoided the collision by a mere inch. Sveinn instantly steadied the rudder, avoiding the side collision too. At this very moment, the Foreign ships crashed into each other right behind their stern.

"Row!" yelled Sveinn.

The Vikings responded instantly, dropping the oars back into the water and pulling hard. Sveinn seized the closest oil lamp and threw it into the burning mess behind.

They did it! Finally daring to exhale, Hrafn joined the Vikings in their triumphant yell. Then he slid down from the mast and walked toward Sveinn, his knees still shaking.

"That was brilliant!" he exclaimed.

Sveinn smirked at him. "Thanks… Four down, three left."

Their maneuver saved Ari's people—when their burning enemy went after Hrafn's ship, they had just enough time to avoid the trap. Instead of being caught between the two enemy boats, they were able to turn to the rocky coastline and get side by side with one of their attackers. The boarding begun, but with rocks behind them, the second Foreign boat could no longer attack them at the same time.

Meanwhile, the third remaining Foreign boat was attacking Hrafn's ship from the left. The Vikings had no more arrows and only a few stones left.

"Get ready to board!" Hrafn shouted, pulling out his sword.

Boarding hooks flew in the air and the loud cracking of broken oars joined the cacophony of menacing yells and screams as the ships approached each other side by side.

"I don't like it," muttered Sveinn. "I don't like it at all…"

Hrafn wanted to ask him what was it that he didn't like, but the fight began and he didn't have time for it.

"Don't leave the ship!" yelled Sveinn. "Let them come!"

Too late: about a dozen of Vikings were already on the Foreign ship, fiercely fighting in the middle of the enemies. Luckily, others heard the order and stayed, meeting the waves of arriving warriors.

The Foreigners obviously outnumbered the Vikings. All of them wore fine helmets and had swords, which spoke of their high rank in their king's army. The Vikings were mostly bareheaded, with only their thick reindeer jackets and wooden shields for protection. Swords were expensive, so most fought with axes, wielding them just as effectively. All of them fought for their own lands, for their homes and families, and this fact only doubled their determination.

Hrafn was still by the rudder. He couldn't move to the heart of the battle yet, so he put the sword down and used the remaining stones, carefully aiming each of them. When all the stones were gone, he grabbed his sword, thinking of the best way to join the battle. Sveinn's voice caught his attention.

"We are trapped. They've got us this time…"

Hrafn looked around and saw what Sveinn meant. They stayed in the center of the wedge, and now the Foreign ship that was unable to attack Ari's was coming for them from the right.

One quick glance at the fighting on the deck told Hrafn that moving away was impossible. Blind panic swept over him, fogging his brain. They were doomed! The prophecy lied; he was unable to win the war! Kirk was right—he was too young and too weak, his skills were too poor to save his own town and defend his own mother!

He clearly saw her lonely, miserable figure crouched on a tree trunk, and her tired, pale face lit by the moonlight. Then he remembered her telling him not to let the panic seize him.

But it was harder to do than it sounded. He forgot how to calm down, the fear growing inside him and paralyzing his limbs. Around him everyone was fighting and it only made him feel even more helpless and panicked. He had to overcome it. Now.

Hrafn closed his eyes focusing on the feel of his father's sword in his hand. The metallic hilt was cold against his skin. He drew a deep breath and projected his thoughts as far as he could, and the familiar, friendly croaking echoed inside him.

He saw the ships from above. Joined in the fight, both vessels looked like a giant anthill where swords, helmets, and shields constantly moved, accompanied by furious growls, groans and yells of pain.

On their right, another Foreign ship readied to board them, pulling on the ropes of their boarding hooks.

Farther away, on the other side of the bay, Ari's crew fought their opponent with a fierce energy.

Also, there was movement at the docks. A new small ship's oars moved rhythmically heading to the right, to their rescue. Olaf had seen Hrafn's signal!

Hrafn's heart gave a happy jolt. Snapping his eyes open,

he shouted, "Everyone back to the ship! Everyone back to the ship!" Then he moved behind the fighters to an open spot by the starboard.

For the first time, he tested his father's sword in real battle. He found that killing people with arrows was easier: moans, blood, and the terrible sight of cut, distorted limbs made him feel sick. But there was no choice—kill or get killed was the only law of the battle. Ignoring his feelings, the boy fought, slaying people, while sweat ran down his back and his forehead. He couldn't tell how long it lasted— warriors kept dying around him, the deck was covered with corpses and limbs, making it difficult to move; he was getting tired and his arms ached.

Sveinn was out of sight, but Kirk appeared by his side, then Ottar. The next moment, he could only see Foreigners around. Right in front of him, a huge, fat Foreigner thrust his sword through Knut's heart. Hrafn helplessly watched Knut's eyes widen in shock and surprise as he lost his last breath. Then his face went pale and his lifeless body fell on the deck.

Horror and pain squeezed the boy's heart, quickly replaced by a sudden and violent thirst of revenge. Letting out an angry growl, he charged on the closest Foreigner. The latter moved back, avoiding the tip of his sword by inches.

But the next moment, the whole ship suddenly shivered, and the warrior was projected forward, receiving Hrafn's sword in the guts. Hrafn lost his balance as well and fell on his back, the dead warrior on top of him. Quickly squirming free, the boy stood and pulled clear his sword. It was no easy task because the hilt was covered with blood and slippery. Fortunately for him, the shock distracted everyone, and no one attacked him before he was ready.

Resuming his fight, Hrafn didn't bother to look around to

find out what was going on. He knew that their enemy on the right had troubles of their own that distracted their attention from his ship.

Indeed, the Foreigners had a real reason to worry—their right side was severely broken and water started filling the hold. Their attacker, a small Viking ship with a heavy, sharply pointed wooden ram attached to the bow, came around for another run. Their shields tied to their backs, the oarsmen rhythmically lifted their twelve pairs of oars. A group of archers shot arrows from the bow, sabotaging all the efforts to fix the broken side.

"Go!" shouted Olaf from the stern, where he pulled the rudder.

His crew instantly plied the oars, hurrying their ship toward their enemy.

A new shock, smaller than the previous one, yet destructive enough shook the Foreign boat and echoed through the adjacent vessels. Foreigners yelled with panic. Most rushed to the starboard side and several Vikings stopped to see what was going on.

"Keep fighting!" shouted Hrafn. "Use their fear!"

Indifferent to spears and arrows mercilessly flying on her, the small ship was already rushing forward for another blow. Another shock, accompanied by a loud crack of broken wood. The Foreign ship was sinking.

"Abandon ship! All to the port! Slay them and get—" yelled the captain. A quick and perfectly aimed arrow from the small ship pierced his throat right between the lower edge of his helmet and the collar of his mail before he could finish. But most warriors heard the order and hurried onto Hrafn's ship.

The Vikings were ready, meeting the coming wave of attackers with axes and swords.

The Foreigners were still too many and they fell like a spring torrent over the Vikings who were now gathered in a group in the middle of their own ship, determined to stand to the end.

Meanwhile, Olaf changed his tactics. Leaving the sinking boat alone, he turned his ship, intending to get to the opposite side of the battle.

The Foreigners didn't notice his maneuver right away, but when they did, a rainfall of arrows and spears fell over the small ship. However, the town's army seemed ready for it: archers crouched behind their shields while oarsmen kept rowing, the shields on their backs protecting them from attack. Small but unstoppable, the ship gained speed, her ram ready for a new victim.

The mere appearance of the small ship on the other side of the battle changed the outcome of the fight: the Foreigners, who mercilessly poured onto Hrafn's ship from both sides, changed direction and hurried to their only remaining ship. Everyone knew that should it sink as well, all of them would be doomed.

When Olaf's ram hit their side, some warriors instantly jumped on the small ship, trying to kill as many people as possible. The oarsmen reversed their stroke, and some Foreigners fell into the water, missing the bow, yet several managed to get in and fought with the archers who had their axes ready at their feet. The arrival of new people unbalanced the small ship whose bow was already too low because of the ram. Her front sank lower, threatening to fill the deck with water.

"Move back!" ordered Olaf, and as his warriors started following, two well-placed archers in the middle killed most of the invaders. The rest were hacked to death with axes and thrown overboard.

The small ship was lucky—only two warriors were wounded so far and no one killed. But Olaf and his crew knew that renewing the attack would mean a nearly sure death for all of them. Their first blow wasn't strong enough—the wood cracked but didn't break. They were well aware of the difference in numbers between the Foreigners and Hrafn's army and they knew they had to help no matter the price. Olaf organized the archers by the stern, leaving only two people on the bow to cover the oarsmen while the ship kept moving away from the battle.

"A bit farther!" he urged the oarsmen. "They must sink!"

Finally, the distance seemed correct.

"Stop!" he yelled and adjusted the rudder.

The oarsmen instantly obeyed.

"Ready? One… two… three!"

All the oars simultaneously hit the water. Taking advantage of the break, the archers readied their bows and placed spare arrows between the teeth. Rowing with all their might, the Vikings flew their small boat at the Foreign ship four times as big. Everyone was silent, frowning with concentration. None of them was scared of death, but they wanted to die with dignity.

The crash was mighty. The wooden side of the Foreigner made a thunderous loud crack as it broke. All three ships shook violently and everyone not braced were sent flying on the deck or overboard.

Olaf instantly ordered to backwater, but a dozen Foreign warriors were on their bow and others rushed to join them. A warrior and two oarsmen were instantly slain. The oarsmen had no choice but to join the fight. They formed a group on the stern, ready to meet the swarming fighters. Olaf seized his bow, positioning himself slightly above the fighting crowd.

"Take that one!" he muttered, sending a deadly arrow into a climbing Foreigner.

Hrafn lost the sense of time and reality. It seemed to him that the chaos of battle would never end. He was in the middle of hell with the crash and clank of weapons, the cacophony of angry roars and yells of pain, the moving bodies, corpses, and blood all around. His limbs were sore and his thoughts stopped, leaving him in a trance where he dodged and struck blows around him. He froze in surprise when, after killing another warrior, he found himself standing by the rail, facing the sinking Foreign ship.

Groups of men still fought, but the Foreigners seemed to be less numerous now. Hrafn blinked in disbelief, spotting his brother's ship nearby. It was crowded with fighting people and Foreigners kept boarding it from their sinking vessel, climbing from all sides. Awakened by the sight, the boy quickly glanced around, thinking. A dagger was stuck in the rail nearby. Hrafn took it and lowered his sword on the deck. Then he hurried over the board to the sinking ship.

Sveinn saw him diving. "Kirk, Örjan, follow me!"

Hrafn swam under water, the dagger in his hand. When he saw the back of a swimming Foreigner in front of him, doubt and fear rose inside him. It was a man, a living being just like himself, and taking his life away seemed so cruel! But then he thought of his brother and his crew that this Foreigner was intending to kill, and all his doubts vanished. Propelling himself forward, he lifted the dagger and hit the man hard on the back. The water turned red with blood. Pulling the dagger free, Hrafn swam toward another enemy.

But that one saw the boy coming. His eyes mad with battle fury, he pulled out a long hunter's knife, ready to fight. Hrafn tightened his grip on the dagger when another Foreigner attacked him from behind.

The boy was lucky: the blow hit the empty scabbard on his back. Abruptly pushed forward, he swallowed a mouthful of salty water. Coughing, he saw his enemy's dagger rise in the air, ready to administer a deadly blow. This time there was no escape.

But instead, someone firmly gripped his shoulder and he was pulled away. His uncle's short sword blocked the Foreigner's knife and sent it flying away. The next moment, the Foreigner was dead.

Distracted by yells, Örjan and Hrafn looked back. The big black raven was furiously attacking the warrior who hit Hrafn at the back. The bird flew around the man's head, pecking at him. The man lost his weapon, yelling in pain and swaying his arms to get rid of the bird. Örjan ended him in one blow and followed Hrafn to the ship. Kirk and Sveinn were already there.

The ship was so jammed with fighters that there was almost no room to fight. She sank too deep and the deck was already filled with water.

Sveinn, Kirk, Hrafn, and Örjan climbed on the bow and fought their way to the middle of the deck. The Foreigners were surrounded. Even though they fought bravely, the Vikings little by little killed most of them. Others jumped into the water, avoiding the swords and daggers. Panting, tired, and covered with blood, the four Vikings finally met the rest of the small ship crew.

"Well done, brother," grinned Hrafn, nodding to Olaf.

The latter wiped his forehead with the sleeve and returned his grin. "Thanks for coming."

But Hrafn was no longer listening. His gaze fell upon the warriors standing next to his brother and his jaw dropped.

"Mother?!"

Kirk, Örjan, and Sveinn were equally surprised.

"Idunn?!" said Sveinn. Hrafn recognized the girl from the neighboring house, with whom Sveinn was flirting.

The two women stood side by side with the young warriors, also wearing thick leather jackets and hats, bows in their hands.

Olaf shrugged at their reaction and explained, "Well, they wanted to come and they proved their skill."

At the sight of her son covered in blood, Turid forgot her warrior side and pushed toward him, determined to take care of his wounds right there.

"Mother, I'm all right..." Hrafn said, embarrassed.

Meanwhile, Sveinn approached Idunn, eying her with curiosity. "So you are a warrior now." he said, smiling. "I like that."

The girl's cheeks flushed, but she stood his glance and answered, "You may be the best swordsman, but you can't beat me with the bow."

"Konungr," called Kirk, using this title for the first time with Hrafn.

Both Olaf and Hrafn turned to look at him.

Kirk was obviously uncomfortable with that, but after their battle he could no longer deny the boy's achievements. "Do we take prisoners?"

Hrafn looked at his brother. "We might need them, huh?"

"Yes, there is a lot to repair."

Twisting his body as much as Turid's firm grip would allow, he turned toward Kirk.

"Take those who are not wounded and those who can be healed!"

The Fortress

Ten days later, both fully repaired ships arrived at the conquered fortress.

It stood in the middle of a sun-burned plain covered with random dry bushes and yellow grass, and seemed lonely and abandoned, like some sort of monastery.

This time, Olaf and all the warriors were there because their ally Brant sent five dozen of his warriors to protect the town and Turid was to assist their chieftain in case of trouble. Hrafn's raven was with him, so he knew before the others that the Foreign army stood already at the fortress's walls.

The Vikings lingered in the sea and arrived at night. They managed to get into the fortress unnoticed by the enemy.

Their fellows in the fortress told them that the Foreigners' army had been there for two days now, but for some reason had not attacked yet. However it looked very big, so the Vikings were expecting an attack any moment.

"We have been waiting for the new konungr to decide what to do here," explained Leif, the Viking who was left in command in the fortress, his eyes flickering toward Hrafn. "If their army is as big as it seems, we have no chance to win."

A war council was called. After some deliberation, it was decided that they didn't have much choice: they had to fight here or the army would follow them to their land and fight them there.

The first prospect seemed more promising—at least, they would fight far from home, keeping the danger away from their families. After they die, the Foreign army would be smaller, so the town might have a chance against them.

Once the decision made, the Vikings started building more catapults and fortifying the walls.

Meanwhile, Olaf and Hrafn were searching the fortress back and forth, looking for something strategic in it.

The whole construction was pretty simple: a rectangular stone building stood in the very center of a large rectangular yard, protected by high stone walls with towers at each corner.

The central building was built over a small natural cavern with a stream of water and several natural pools, wide enough for a man to take a bath there. Thanks to the stream, the water in the pools was constantly renewed, evacuating through a series of small natural underground passages.

The central building had a kitchen with a fireplace, a privy next to the outgoing water stream, and six sleeping rooms on the second floor.

The yard was dry and empty. Three lonely trees grew in a small garden by the main building, while stables, chicken coop, smithy, storehouses, and other work-related premises ran alongside the fortress walls.

"There must be something vital for them here!" stated Hrafn for the thousand and fifth time.

Olaf leaned on the stone wall. "We searched every stone and there is nothing!"

"Obviously, because we found nothing!" said Hrafn, irritated. "Or we found something, but didn't pay attention to it! Otherwise, why aren't they attacking?"

Olaf approached the edge of the wall and spat down. He watched his spittle fly all the way down the wall and fall on a gray sunlit stone. The air was hot and motionless, and on the other side of the wall, all the grass was dry and yellow.

"Look, Hrafn, it's so hot that the spittle cooked away!"

Forgetting for a moment about the fortress, Hrafn peered down from the top of the wall as his brother repeated the experiment.

"Ha!" he exclaimed and spat as well.

"Nay, mine lasted longer!" stated Olaf.

"It can't be!"

"Yes, it did!"

"It's water, all the same!"

"Nope! I'm telling you, I saw it!"

"Liar!"

"No, I'm not!"

"Yes, you are!" Hrafn pushed him in the shoulder.

Olaf laughed and then suggested, "Let's spit together, all right. You'll see... you'll see!"

Frowning, Hrafn stood next to his brother and they took aim.

His eyes eagerly sparkling, Olaf counted with firm gestures and they spat down on the very same flat grey stone. Two dark dots appeared there and the boys bent as low as they could, apprehensively observing whose one would disappear first. But Olaf was right: Hrafn's spittle started getting smaller and smaller, while Olaf's was still clearly visible. Then it just vanished, leaving Hrafn slightly pissed off.

Olaf gave out a triumphant laugh.

"So who is a liar now?"

Hrafn straightened his back, intending to respond. But a white spot on the horizon drew his attention. A white flag lazily moved in the hot breeze over the Foreign camp.

The boy blinked in disbelief.

By that time, Olaf spotted the flag as well, and his amazement was just the same. "The white flag? They want to parley?"

But Hrafn was already running downstairs, jumping two steps at once.

"We accept!" he shouted back to Olaf.

Ari was running toward him. "Are you intending to parley?"

"Find something white for our own flag! Find Sveinn as well!"

"I'm here," Sveinn answered calmly from behind, putting his hand on the boy's shoulder. "Honored by your trust. If you want my advice, do not answer too soon, or they'll think we are fearful."

"You're right," he said. "Olaf! Come down here! Ottar, keep the guard."

Soon Olaf, Hrafn, Sveinn, Ari, Orm, Leif, Kirk, and other Vikings gathered in the yard, in the shade of the central building.

"... we crushed seven of their boats and the fortress can protect us," Olaf was saying. "We have enough rocks to destroy half of their army."

"Don't underestimate them," interrupted Hrafn. "They outnumber us more than ten times!"

Ari said, "I've been to some talks with Torgeir. Normally, they just want to threaten us before attacking. Filthy dogs! The best thing to do is to go out there and to threaten them first! They must know that we're not cowards!" His clenched fist heavily landed on his own palm and Hrafn winced, imagining the pain of such a blow. "We have never run away from a fight!"

"Aye, never!" caught a chorus of proud angry voices.

"We'll fight again no matter how few we are, and I swear, I'll take with me as many of these scum as possible!" declared Leif, hitting his chest with both his fists.

A roar of approval met his words.

Hrafn was a Viking too and thus could not disagree with them, yet he wasn't sure that was the best way to do it. He said, "There was no question of running away, we are here and will fight here. Orm, Sveinn, what do you think?"

"I think we'd better avoid the threats and negotiate with them. What if they have a valuable proposition? After all, we don't have to answer right away," said Orm.

"Proposition?!" choked Ari. "They were the first to attack our lands! You've seen what they've done: they burned entire villages, keeping no prisoners at all, killing all, killing children and women! They devastated everything! Do you really believe that now they will just confess they've had enough? That they'll just go home and leave us in peace?! I'm telling you, man, their best proposition will sound like 'surrender now before we pull your hearts off and feed them to our dogs'! Their king's name means 'wolf' for a good reason!"

Everyone around him fell silent. They remembered but too well what made the Vikings go to war, knowing that they were so outnumbered from the very beginning.

Hrafn had difficulty to remain calm, but he reminded himself that they needed to discuss all the possibilities. He turned toward Orm and asked, "Suppose we accept to talk. But if we go back to think over every question of theirs, won't they think we are cowards?"

Orm just shrugged. "Cowards? I don't think so. They may think we are stupid and long to react, which only suits us. But they are smarter than that. They will expect us to do so, and if they don't, it will only confuse them."

"Well, that makes it easier," grinned Hrafn. "What do you think, brother?"

Olaf nodded.

Ari's brows pulled together and he was about to argue further, but Hrafn turned toward Sveinn who had not said a word and asked, "What about you, Sveinn?"

"I agree with Orm," Sveinn said. "We don't seem to have too much choice. If we listen first, we might find out something useful and then come up with a better answer. I'm not saying it is going to be so, but I believe it worth a try."

"Nonsense!" cut across him Ari. "They'll just kill our messenger! It's a sacrifice for nothing!"

Sveinn just sighed. "It could be, or it could not. Until we go, we'll never find out. I know I'm willing to take the risk."

The furrow between Ari's brows deepened. He squared his massive shoulders with pride, getting ready to respond to the offense. But Sveinn did not intend to be rude. His both palms flying upwards in an apologetic gesture, he hurried to add, "Look, I'm not saying that you're wrong! May be you're damn right! But I'm curious, that's my nature." Then he turned to Hrafn, finishing his thought, "Also, I think that if you do it, you'd better send a man for it. No offense, Konungr, but they won't take you or your brother seriously."

But Hrafn was far from being offended. "I would like *you* to go," he confessed. "You are wise enough not to lose your temper before it is needed."

"Good idea!" agreed Orm. "Should you send Ari, he will kill the messenger before the poor man speaks!"

Ari crossed his arms over his chest and snorted.

Sveinn nodded. "As you order."

Hrafn was sure he saw a new, eager sparkle in the dark depth of Sveinn's eyes.

The Talks

A white flag was raised and a side gate was opened, letting Sveinn out to meet the Foreign messenger. Despite the heat, Sveinn wore his thick reindeer jacket and his sword hung on his back. Calm as usual, he rode toward the messenger.

From the top of the wall, Orm, Olaf, and Hrafn watched as both negotiators stopped several feet from each other. To everyone's amazement, Sveinn respectfully greeted the Foreigner, and the latter greeted him back.

"Aye, Sveinn!" muttered Orm, grinning into his gray beard. "What a man!"

Then they saw the Foreigner speak. Sveinn nodded and answered. Then he turned his horse and rode back. The Foreigner remained where he was, by the white flag stuck into the dry ground.

They hurried down to meet Sveinn.

When the gate closed behind him, Sveinn started speaking without dismounting his horse. "Their king wants us to hear the following: 'Torgeir, my army counts ten times more men than this fortress can hold. You may have destroyed seven of my ships, but you lost a lot of warriors as well, and I can wipe from the earth's face this fortress and all of you with my catapults alone. If you are wise and if you value the life of your warriors, take your last opportunity and leave now. In my infinite kindness, I promise that we will let all of you go, if you disappear and leave everything intact. Otherwise, we will torture and kill every single one of you and your ships will become my trophies.'"

"That filthy dog is lying!" growled Ari, clenching his fists.

"No, he's not," retorted Hrafn. "His army really is that big."

"How do you know? He might just have put two lines of warriors alongside the horizon to make us believe they are too many!"

"I know and I'm sure! But it doesn't matter… any ideas for further actions?"

"Ten times! Well, we don't really have any arguments to oppose them," mused Kirk. "We accept their conditions and die fighting."

"What's the use of it?" intervened Orm. "They kill all of us and then they are free to keep the lands they stole from us and to attack our town again. But this time, there will be only five dozens of Brant's people to resist them. They will keep going. conquering all our neighbors one by one, as they always wanted!"

Everyone fell silent. Then Olaf stated, "He still believes father's alive."

Hrafn kicked a stone under his feet and swore. "If only we knew the secret of this damned fortress!"

"We don't really need to know it," mused Sveinn, looking at the boy with narrowed eyes.

"Yes, we do!" retorted Hrafn. "It could have been an important asset to us!"

"It still is an important asset."

Hrafn stared at him. "You mean... we bluff?"

Sveinn nodded and started ticking on his fingers. "First, until now they haven't attacked though they can easily win. Second, they want us to leave without destruction, which can only mean the fortress. Third, they have announced us the exact number of their warriors. To me our assets look obvious."

Still bewildered, Hrafn nodded. "So, we'll just pretend we know it…"

Sveinn straightened. An eager sparkle shone in his dark, long-lashed eyes. "What can we lose anyway? Let me go and talk to them!"

Hrafn threw a quick glance at the others, but no one showed any objection.

"Go," he said. "I cannot think of someone who talks as well as you do."

"Good. Wait until everyone is in place."

~~~

Sveinn rode back to the king's messenger.

The latter was obviously losing his patience in the early-afternoon heat while Sveinn looked calm and impassive. Stopping his horse several paces from the Foreigner, he politely thanked him for waiting and announced, "This is what my King wants me to tell your King: Foreign King, how dare you talk to me about wisdom when you are stupid enough to underestimate your enemy? You are so childish and pathetic bragging of your army that we cannot see how you got a reputation as a brave warrior. Even our children laugh at you! But as you gave me the advantage of knowing your strengths, I will do the same: know, Ulfrich, that the army I have here is four times smaller than yours, but it is more than enough to do what it takes to destroy all of you, for we have magic and we know why the fortress we are holding is important to you!"
~~~

Sveinn stated those deeply offensive words in a firm, even voice and watched the effect with hidden satisfaction. It worked just as he had expected: first the messenger went bright pink with fury and clenched his fists, but at the mention of the fortress, the man's went pale, and Sveinn interpreted it as a very good sign.

The Foreigner didn't answer. He turned his horse and galloped toward his camp.

Sveinn was left alone by the flag in his turn. Trying to look as at ease as possible, he waited. The burning sun mercilessly heated his thick jacket and the motionless air made the heat more unbearable. But Sveinn was an excellent warrior. Straight and proud, he remained in his saddle while the sense of danger he was playing with tickled his nerves. That was how he liked it—carefully bouncing at the very edge of the abyss, risking it all.

Finally, the messenger appeared. He was so tense, fighting back his rage that his horse danced uneasily. He shouted, "King Torgeir, if you are as strong as you pretend to be clever, and if you have the nerve and the daring, meet me in a fair sword fight. No help and no magic, just you and me, king to king!"

Sveinn remained impassive, but this turn surprised him: the Foreigner was informed that Torgeir's weakest weapon was the sword, or he must have been an excellent swordsman. Anyway, Sveinn's intuition told him that a trick was to be expected there.

Nodding to show he understood, he turned his horse and rode back to the fortress.

"He wants a duel!" gasped Olaf. "Well, that could be a perfect solution!"

"Verily," nodded Sveinn. "If we eliminate every possibility of him playing a trick on us."

"Well, we can, can't we?" answered Hrafn. "We accept the duel, if he and his successors swear on their goddess of Earth in front of everybody that the duel will decide the outcome of the war. They are superstitious and their gods mean a lot to them."

"You mean…" began Jari.

"If he loses," explained the boy, his emerald eyes shining, "they give back our lands and swear not to attack us again, and if he wins… well, we fight until we die. Anyway, they will never let us go. I say that's our only chance."

Everyone stared, too bewildered to speak.

Ari shook his head. "No one will ever guarantee the peace forever. Their king's got family and they will avenge his death, without speaking of their reasons for conquering our lands in the first place."

"Well, we can ask for ten winters then," suggested Olaf. "In ten winters we can grow our fleet and army and find new allies."

"That sounds more plausible," agreed Leif. "Though they can do the same."

"The stake is too big," said Orm, shaking his head. "He will certainly make us swear that we will surrender without fighting, if he wins…"

Hrafn shrugged. "We have to try. If they attack and kill us, they will rule over us anyway. But less people will die, if we reduce the war to a duel."

Ari's eyes bulged. He was now persuaded that the boy had gone mad. "I'd rather die fighting than surrender and live to see them take my land!" he exclaimed angrily.

"Do you see another solution?" asked Olaf.

Ari wanted to protest, but he didn't have anything to suggest, so he sighed angrily and closed his mouth, crossing his arms over his chest.

Finally, Sveinn rode back to the messenger.

"My King tells that he accepts the fair sword fight between the two of them, without magic or help, but the duel must decide the outcome of the war—if my King wins, you give us our lands back and swear in the name of your supreme goddess that none of your people will attack us for the next ten years."

The Foreigner looked surprised and Sveinn couldn't tell whether it was because the request was too daring, or for some other reason. Sharply turning his horse, the man galloped away.

Keeping his impassive expression, Sveinn readied himself to die. The messengers were usually the first to experience the discontent of rulers. He recalled his life with all the good and bad things, his native town, that attractive Idunn he didn't have time to properly flirt with... He did not fear death, but waiting for it was a trial.

When the messenger returned, Sveinn was ready to seize his sword.

A mocking sneer twisted the corners of the messenger's lips. "Tell your king that my King agrees. But if he wins, you all surrender and he will rule over you and your lands! He is coming right here, to the flag. Be ready!"

Sveinn nodded and galloped away, still expecting a spear or an arrow to hit him in the back. But he reached the fortress safe and hurried to announce the news.

"I told you these talks were a bad idea!" complained Ari. "They want us to surrender! What a shame! To take our lands without fighting!"

"It is worth a try," disagreed Orm. "We can still win!"

"If we make the oath the right way, we can omit the part about not fighting back," suggested Leif. "That way we will only risk one warrior."

Hrafn only half-listened. He removed his scabbard and put his thick reindeer jacket over his shirt. Then he gathered and checked his shield and his sword. The plan was already shimmering in his mind, and he let it form by itself and come.

Ari's eyes widened. "Konungr, what are you doing? Don't you think of going to fight him! They don't know Torgeir is dead! We can send them someone who looks like your father!"

This time, Hrafn was offended. "I am the konungr and I gave my word!"

"But he is older and stronger!" continued Ari, obviously worried.

Hrafn looked heavenward. "I know!"

"How is that?" intervened Kirk sarcastically. "Another prophetic dream?"

"From the wall!" Hrafn snapped. "Just like Ottar!"

"You can't go to that duel!" exclaimed Ari, exasperated.

Hrafn's eyes narrowed. "Why not? I'm too small and too weak? Well, that's even better—if I get killed all the worthy warriors will remain unharmed! Anyway, none of you are happy to see me as a new konungr!"

Everyone watched him in silence. They could not deny that last point.

"There is no time for arguing!" sighed Orm. "We need a plan. Now."

"I have one." Still fuming, Hrafn laced his jacket and looked at them. "We know for sure that the Foreigners are very superstitious and afraid of magic, just like we know that their main goddess is the goddess of Earth. We need to win this battle by all means. So here is what I think we should do…"

Wolf versus Raven

The Vikings left the fortress in a group with Ari, Orm, Sveinn, Kirk, and Leif riding first.

"He must swear first, before he discovers I'm the konungr!" insisted Hrafn.

Behind them, the fortress was silent. The remaining Vikings stood by the catapults observing the little group of riders through Ottar, who stood watch at the wall. They were ready to attack at the slightest sign of the Foreigners' dishonesty.

The riders stopped before the Foreign army and Orm called, "Say your vow, Foreign King, you and your possible successors!"

The king proudly straightened. He was huge, even by Viking measures. His muscles seemed unnatural and made him look trollish. He wore a mail hauberk and his long brown hair was caught in a thin ponytail, under the metal plates of his helmet. Even his horse was taller and broader than all the others, apparently a rare animal brought from afar.

Disdainful, the Foreigner spoke. Hrafn understood most of it, for he had spent time learning their language from his prisoners. Ulfrich announced his titles and swore on his supreme goddess, the goddess of Earth, that they will fight one on one, no help and no magic, and if he lost, he would return the lands he conquered from Torgeir and not attack for the next ten years.

Two other warriors repeated the same after their king, each strong and proud.

It was Hrafn's turn now. Trying to remember their phrasing, he urged his horse forward and stopped before his warriors.

"I am Konungr Hrafn, son of Torgeir the Brave," he announced. "I accept your conditions and swear by Odin, my supreme God—"

A thunderous burst of laughter from a hundred of warriors swallowed the sound of his voice. Quickly recovering from their surprise, Ulfrich's men shook, bending in two and pointing their fingers at the boy. The air trembled with their deep roars of laughter.

Still Hrafn forced himself to go on, pretending he didn't notice. "—that if I lose, my people and my lands will—"

The laughter grew louder, and Hrafn stopped, omitting all the rest. It could not have been worse if every one of them had spat at him. He endured it, though his face turned red. Struggling with all his might to keep his face straight, he waited for them to calm down.

Wiping the tears of laughter, Ulfrich finally said, "Are you intending to fight me, boy? Go back to your mommy and wipe that milk from your lips!"

Another fit of laughter shook the Foreigners.

Hrafn clenched his fists so tight that his knuckles went white. "Shame on you, Foreigner!" he shouted. "*I* have destroyed your mighty fleet! A boy! Want to see your sailors among my slaves? They taught me your tongue!"

Ulfrich stopped laughing. He considered Hrafn and then proudly lifted his chin. "Find someone worthy for the task." he threw disdainfully. "I won't fight a child!"

Hrafn drew a deep, rasping breath. It was all or nothing now, and no turning back. "Are you afraid that I will win? You waited for many days, not daring attack the fortress with only three dozen of men inside, and now you try to avoid a fight with a boy! Aren't you a coward after that?"

This time Ulfrich's face went bright red with fury. No one laughed now.

The boy sensed the unrest of his men, whose unblinking stares bore into his back.

"All right then, boy…" said the Foreigner. "I'll fight you one on one, as I swore. When I win, I'll tear you to pieces and throw them to my dogs. Then I'll make a big feast and burn your warriors alive! Get ready!"

Ulfrich dismounted his horse, leaving it with the warriors, then gathered his shield and removed his sword from the scabbard. He strode to the bald patch of earth surrounded by the low dry bushes where the duel would take place, far enough from both armies to make sure the fight was really one on one.

Meanwhile, Hrafn did the same.

"You know what to do," he threw to Olaf. "Just make sure no one sees you."

Completely hidden under an elaborate rag disguise and surrounded by tall warriors, Olaf nodded. He couldn't talk— a thick curtain of tears blurred his view, and his voice would surely have given him away.

Hrafn hurriedly looked away, feeling too much like crying, too.

Sveinn grasped his arm. His face was paler than usual. "Konungr, my sword is lighter. Take it, if you want!"

Hrafn just shook his head. "No, thanks. I'm just not used to it." His father's sword at the ready, he walked to the place of duel.

"Stay calm and save your strength!" advised Sveinn from behind, and Hrafn desperately clung to these words.

To say he was scared was an understatement. A part of him was regretting his foolish bargain, but it was too late to turn back. The agreement was sealed. He wished that Sveinn could have given him more lessons, or that he was older or that less were at stake.

Stay calm and save your strength! he repeated inside his head. He would do his best. The plan was very simple, inspired by the rune caster's prophecy. Hrafn's part was to fight, giving time for everyone to get in place, and to die fighting, like a hero. Then Olaf was to come out and do the most dangerous job—play Hrafn's resurrection and kill Ulfrich while he would not expect it. Two young Vikings, Vali and Helgi, were to make Hrafn's body disappear by any means and as quickly as possible. Then there would be only two possible outcomes: the Foreigners would honor their oath or the Vikings would fight, as no oath was given to restrain them.

Knowing what was about to come, the raven bird uttered a heartbreaking, sorrowful croak from high above. But Hrafn didn't look up. The raven had a special task—to inform him when everyone was ready—and Hrafn had his own. His death stood by his side, and he had to make it linger. Only for a short while, then his task would be over and he would be out of the fight forever. He was named konungr to win the war, and he had to do so by any possible means. Well, it wouldn't be exactly himself who would win, but then it wouldn't really matter.

The end was so close that he could no longer tell whether he wanted it over faster, or whether he wanted it to last— just to live a bit longer, to steal a couple of heartbeats from death itself.

He had never been so much aware of everything around him—the heat, the air, the burning sun, the dry land, and yellow grass, people's stares fixed upon him, his raven flying somewhere above it all… Hrafn was about to leave it forever and it was now so frighteningly real.

Forcing his heavy feet to move, he focused on Ulfrich. It was crucial for the success of their foolish plan.

He stopped before Ulfrich who adjusted his long shield, mockingly smiling down. Hrafn barely reached his chest!

"Did you hug everyone good-bye?" said Ulfrich. Amused, he added louder, so that everyone would hear "We are not cowards! We will honor our oath even though the foolish Viking baby-king made it so easy for us. So be it, let him play before he dies!"

"Aye!" replied the chorus of voices.

Hrafn swallowed and added in a gruff voice, "If I kill you, it will be my pleasure to ride your horse. A fair beast for a king."

Ulfrich lifted his sword, indicating the beginning of the battle.

His first swing was rough and strong, obviously to kill a weak and poorly-skilled opponent. Hrafn easily dodged away and attacked back, swiping at Ulfrich's legs. He only cut the laces of the Foreigner's left shoe, without even scratching him, and it provoked another fit of laughter from the crowd.

However, action freed Hrafn from his fear, finally allowing him to focus.

Ulfrich tried other simple blows and each could easily kill a grown man. But light and small, the boy avoided them as well. Losing his patience, the giant changed his tactics to more elaborate ones.

Ulfrich was an excellent swordsman. His attacks were quick and skillful, and his blows hard. His massive size allowed him to cover a lot of space, to the disadvantage of his small opponent.

Poor Hrafn was forced to jump and madly twist his body to avoid his enemy's sword. He could no longer think of attacking; all of his focus was on staying alive for as long as possible. Even the roar of the crowd now seemed to come from very far.

A swing to the right. Hrafn blocked with his shield. Jump. Drop. Block again. Another swing. Turn. Jump again. A feint attack! Hrafn dodged at the very last moment. Ulfrich's sword sliced past his temple, nearly touching his skin. The move cost him his balance and he fell to one knee. Ulfrich's sword flashed under the sun, rushing toward his head. The boy instinctively covered himself with the shield.

The blow came like a peal of thunder, making the boy's knee sink deeply into the ground. His shield broke in two and Ulfrich's sword made a cut in his left shoulder. His eyes screwed with pain, Hrafn blindly swung his sword and was surprised to hear Ulfrich's howl.

The boy fell on the ground and rolled away, then hurriedly jumped to his feet. He had wounded the Foreigner on the knee.

One quick glance through his raven's eyes told him that Olaf was still some ten paces from the covering bushes. Throwing the useless piece of his broken shield away, Hrafn ducked from another furious swing. This time, Ulfrich was really angry.

They kept fighting: Hrafn dodging, Ulfrich attacking. The sun mercilessly burned the plain, making the fighters sweat, and the audience from both sides felt more and more restless. The Foreigners urged their king to finish the boy faster. As for the Vikings, they remained silent, following Hrafn's every move and afraid even to breathe.

The wounded shoulder hurt terribly, hampering his movements. Hrafn's whole arm went limp and waves of weariness washed over him. His shirt went red with blood, but so did Ulfrich's trousers. The Foreigner's steps became uneven, but he still fought remarkably and Hrafn had more and more trouble avoiding his sword, especially given that he no longer had his shield to protect him. Time slowed as his limbs grew heavier and the heat made it difficult to breathe. He knew his death was only a couple of heartbeats away now and was surprised to be still on his feet. Feeling that he wouldn't last much longer, he mentally urged Olaf, Vali, and Helgi to move faster.

Then, Sveinn's voice distinctively came out of the humming in his head. "Attack! Hrafn, attack!"

Somehow gathering his thoughts, he made a feint.

The king stepped to the left, leaving his right unprotected. Hrafn instantly dived under Ulfrich's arm. He swiveled around and hit the king on the right side with all his might.

His blade met Ulfrich's fine hauberk and the shock made his whole arm go numb. Ulfrich's angry snarl died away, for Hrafn's blow left him breathless. Ulfrich spun around and his sword hit Hrafn's at the hilt, and sent it flying. The boy's eyes widened as he watched his sword make a half-turn in the air, glittering in the sun, to fall on the grass somewhere behind Ulfrich.

Anticipating what was to come, Hrafn fell back just in time to avoid the returning swing, and quickly rolled away from his enemy.

Standing, he felt dizzy and swayed, nearly losing his balance.

How long am I going to last? he thought desperately.

Ulfrich saw his weakness. His sword painfully hit the boy on the back, but the thick jacket saved him. Hrafn jumped away from another blow, his legs shaking. And finally the long-awaited croak echoed in the air, telling the boy that everyone was in place. He was free to die. Closer to his death than he had ever been, Hrafn remembered in a flash what he had once been told: he would never be accepted to Valhalla if he died without his sword!

Fighting back a new fit of dizziness, he decided to get to it at any price. He avoided the next blow by pure luck and flung himself forward, passing between the Foreigner's powerful legs.

His foot got caught on dry roots and he fell flat on the hard, dry ground. Grass picked his face and neck, and he groaned as the tips of his fingers hit the blade of his sword.

This time it was really over. Both Hrafn and Ulfrich felt it. Ulfrich spun around, a triumphant yell on his lips. His sword flashed in the sun, raised for the final blow. He lifted his good leg to step toward his victim, not noticing that he was standing on his loose laces. The next moment, he fell over the boy prostrated at his feet, his triumphant yell echoing through the plain.

Hrafn didn't want to die. No matter what people said, he loved life very much. In that very instant, only a heartbeat before his unavoidable death, Hrafn understood it. It was more an urge, a primitive instinct, than a conscious action, but he couldn't resist it. He rolled to the back and held the sword in front of him parallel to the ground. He screwed his eyes shut and thrust the sword up with both hands just as Ulfrich's heavy body crashed over him, burying him underneath.

The pain was such that he saw stars. Hrafn was smashed and the shock kicked the breath out of his chest. The last thing he felt was Ulfrich's helmet jabbing his face. Then the darkness closed above him.

The Secret of the Fortress

Blood. Blood was everywhere. He felt it running down his face and on his lips. He felt its unpleasant, salty taste on his tongue while its metallic smell filled his nostrils, making his stomach heave.

He couldn't breathe and his whole body writhed in the grip of burning pain. So that was death? But wasn't it supposed to be peaceful and painless?

His arms sore and shaking, he still clutched the blade of his sword. Slowly freeing his right arm, Hrafn wiped his eyes with his sleeve and blinked them open, bringing the world into focus. It took him some time to realize what had just happened; when it finally dawned, he felt sick. He twisted his body, ignoring the pain, in a desperate struggle to free himself.

Ulfrich's heavy body lay over him, pressing him into the ground. Blood gushed from the deep cut in his throat where Hrafn's outstretched sword was still deeply stuck.

Groaning and fighting against a fit of sickness, the boy struggled to free himself from under the dead weight of muscles and metal. He desperately needed some fresh air.

But the task happened to be very difficult. When he already assumed that he would die there, under his enemy's dead body, he finally managed to free his chest.

The air rushed to his lungs and he let himself fall down

on the grass, savoring the feeling of being able to breathe and live again. He waited for the black spots blurring his view to vanish. It felt so good just to lie there motionless and breathe with his full chest that he would have remained like that, but Olaf's worried whisper brought him back to reality.

"Hrafn! ... Hrafn! You're alive?"

Thoughts swirled in his exhausted brain and he answered, "Looks like it."

His raven impatiently croaked somewhere above his head, urging him to get up as a konungr was supposed to. It was not over yet, and everyone was waiting for him.

"Move away, but stay hidden," he whispered to Olaf, Vali, and Helgi. None of them had thought of such an outcome, so they had to improvise now.

Suppressing a groan, Hrafn leaned on his good arm and pushed himself up. When he sat, he felt dizzy again.

Come on! he urged himself. *The worst is over!*

Pulling out his legs seemed endless and desperate, and when he finally succeeded, he was completely exhausted. The black raven soared down and landed on the ground next to him.

"All right, all right," muttered the boy and gathered his father's sword, sticky with blood. Leaning on it, he struggled to his feet and looked around.

Pale-faced and worried, the Vikings stared back at him. On the opposite side from them, the Foreigners remained just as motionless and silent.

Hrafn swallowed. He suddenly realized what an unexpected turn the events had taken. Forgetting for a moment that he was sick and giddy, he blinked, staring with wide eyes at Ulfrich's motionless body. How could that be? Ulfrich dead? The sight of Ulfrich's mighty figure with a triumphant grin and raised glittering sword was still too clear in Hrafn's mind. The giant's death was unbelievable. Maybe his imagination was playing tricks on him? Hrafn touched his own body. It felt hard and real...and in pain. Still, he couldn't believe his incredible luck.

Seeing his bewilderment, the black raven hoped toward him and slightly pecked at his calf.

"*See, you're alive,*" the bird announced, silently answering the boy's surprised face. "*Don't think of how you did it, just play along, Konungr.*"

Bemused, Hrafn nodded. Leaning on his sword, he lifted his clenched fist over his head in victory.

The Vikings erupted into yells of triumph. They couldn't believe it either, but the stake was too important for them, and no one bothered to hide their joy.

As for the Foreigners, they kept staring silently, without moving.

After a moment of expectant hesitation, Ulfrich's brothers who had said the oath with him stepped forward and walked toward Hrafn.

The boy tensed. He wouldn't be able to fight them, he was barely able to stand. But he knew it had to be done. They had to see whether Ulfrich was really dead.

Somehow Hrafn managed to move clear of Ulfrich's dead body to give the men room and to put some distance between them and himself.

When the Foreigners stepped into the bald patch on which the duel took place, the Vikings froze expectantly. Olaf, Vali, and Helgi crouched behind the low bushes observing the scene. They were ready to intervene instantly if the need should arise.

But the Foreigners were suspicious, too. They stopped by Ulfrich's body. One of them crouched to examine it while the other stood alert, eyeing Hrafn with hatred.

"It's unbelievable!" exclaimed the first man. "He's dead!"

He, too, looked at Hrafn, anger and fury distorting his face, and slowly stood.

Hrafn's heart beat so loud, he was sure both Foreigners could hear it. His stomach writhed; he forgot about his pain and weariness. He was scared now. Really scared. His miraculous victory would be for nothing should they decide not to honor their part of the agreement. Moreover, he was at their mercy, alone and badly wounded.

"Don't quail now!" rang the raven's sharp order in his head. The bird hid from the Foreigners' sight in the bush, just behind Hrafn. It eased some of the boy's emotions.

Hrafn instantly felt better, straightened his back, and proudly lifted his chin.

"We fought fairly and I won," he stated calmly and firmly. "Now honor your oath."

The Foreigners didn't move, their fists clenched and their nostrils flaring with fury.

"What makes you think that we must honor it, puppy?" sneered the eldest of them.

Hrafn's mind worked hard, selecting the right words. He settled for the easiest. "Your goddess. She will punish you otherwise."

"You know nothing of our goddess, you filthy..." indignantly began the youngest Foreigner.

He never ended his sentence. Loud angry croaks covered his voice and vibrated through the battlefield as Hrafn's black raven rose in the air. For the time of one breath, the raven flapped its powerful wings, suspending itself over Hrafn's head. Then it screeched and menacingly spread its wings, rushing toward the Foreigners. Both men instinctively moved out of its way.

The raven screeched again, a horrible sound that made

the hairs stand on the back of every neck, and flew at the Foreign army. Fast and furious, with its jet-black eyes and its open beak, the bird looked like some sort of demon or dark spirit, seeking retribution. The Foreigners shivered and gasped, moving away.

The raven passed right above their heads, casting its fierce shadow upon them, but not touching anyone. Then, after another series of loud croaks, it disappeared in the bushes, behind the Foreigners who followed it with frightened glances.

Ulfrich's brothers slowly turned back to Hrafn. They looked paler than before and even their fury seemed to have faded.

The eldest swallowed and curtly said, "We will honor our oath. We will call our people from your lands and we will not attack you for the next ten years. Now leave our lands. You can go unharmed."

The war was over. He won. Hrafn swallowed and nodded.

"We will leave right after your men are gone from our lands. Until then, we won't be seeking fight, but we won't spare attackers either."

Hrafn's next challenge was to walk back. He expected his knees to buckle any moment and was very much relieved when, after he made a couple of shaky steps, the Vikings finally surrounded him.

"They will honor their oath," Hrafn told them. He wanted to tell them the rest, but his voice was completely covered by happy exclamations and congratulations. Familiar bearded faces beamed at him from all sides, shining with pride and relief.

"Good fight!" congratulated Ari.

"You did it!"

"Well done!" added Orm.

"It's just luck!" stammered Hrafn, embarrassed by that many compliments.

"Luck often comes to those who are brave," retorted Sveinn.

Finally, Olaf was there too. Thick tears poured down his cheeks, but he was beaming. "You… you…" he mumbled, unable to gather his thoughts, nor to find his voice.

Hrafn gave him a weak smile. He had one very urgent problem to solve.

"Catch me before I fall," he mouthed. Olaf's gray eyes darkened but he reacted quickly. He stepped on Hrafn's good side and passed his arm around his brother's waist. Hrafn sighed and thankfully leaned on him.

Kirk made his way to the boys and to everyone's amazement, bowed deeply. "Sorry for doubting you, Konungr…" he mumbled, his face pink. "You were… brilliant!"

Hrafn smiled at him. "Thanks, Kirk… I appreciate it."

Back in the fortress, Sveinn took care of Hrafn's shoulder, while Jari brought him some food and water. It had its effect instantly—the dizziness disappeared, leaving only dull pain and heavy weakness in his whole body.

"You know, Konungr," said Sveinn, cleaning the deep cut. "I guess I'll have to teach you from now on. You have my word."

A happy grin lit the boy's scratched and dirty face. Sveinn only raised an eyebrow. "When your arm is healed, of course."

Hrafn wanted to thank him, but Olaf broke into the room, a jar of water in his hands. "I found it!" he shouted excitedly. "I found the secret of the fortress!"

Everyone turned to look at him.

Showing all of his teeth in a happy smile, Olaf strode toward the table and put the jar on it.

"Water!" he said simply. "The fortress is their main water source!"

Going Home

The bright midday sun made the curved blue spines of the waves impossibly shiny and pleasantly warmed the wooden deck of the Viking ship.

Fully enjoying this warmth, Olaf and Hrafn took their meal on the stern by the rudder, their backs leaning on the gunwales and their legs stretched. Hrafn's raven ate its portion of food next to its master.

"Feels good going home!" sighed Hrafn, sliding even lower to get more sun on his body.

"Hmm…" agreed his brother, chewing his bread with appetite.

Hrafn yawned and closed his eyes, silently enjoying the moment and the sensations.

"So the rune caster saw it right—you did win the war." Olaf mused.

Hrafn shrugged lazily. "I'm so glad it did happen. Can't tell you how nervous I felt about it!"

"Yeah, but it means that the second part is very likely to happen as well," he said gloomily.

Hrafn gave him an inquiring glance. "So what?"

Olaf straightened, his gaze fixed on his brother, and frowned.

"Well… aren't you… upset about it?" he muttered.

Hrafn chuckled. "Upset? About what?" he reached out to

give his raven another piece of meat. "If I get it right, I'm one of the luckiest men on earth because I'm going to meet my true love!" He snickered and leaned back against the wooden board of the ship.

Olaf frowned more. "Yeah, but you're going to lose her... I'll be avenging you because of her!"

Hrafn lazily scratched the tip of his nose and stated, a mysterious smile playing at the corners of his lips, "Don't worry, I've got a plan: once I find her, I'll keep her with me for as long as I can, and then I'll act like a man and make sure she gets less suffering than me—remember, the rune caster said there was a choice to be made?"

Olaf nodded, still frowning.

"Well, that's my choice, brother," Hrafn suppressed a yawn and added, "I'll just try to get the best out of it."

Olaf was far from being convinced even as he watched Hrafn's dreamy expression. Shaking his head with obvious disapproval, he said, "Look, the rune caster said destiny can be changed. Why don't you just make sure you never meet her and live a long and happy life?"

Hrafn rolled his eyes at him. "No! ... I want to find her! I'm curious; so few people have such a chance!"

Olaf sighed. "But what if the price is too high? He said there will be a lot of suffering. What if a lot is too much to bear?"

Hrafn dismissively waved his hand. "I'll take my chances. It's my destiny, after all, and I'm fine with it."

Olaf sulked. It still seemed totally ridiculous to him.

Observing him from under his lashes, Hrafn saw it and suppressed a smile. He patted his brother's shoulder and muttered, "Now that the war's over, we can do something interesting. We can practice a lot and defeat Sveinn. Or we can come up with some new hunting methods because winter is approaching. And remember, you wanted to make a flying snake?…"

The last words made Olaf's eyes shine.

"Yes!" he whispered excitedly, but then stopped. "But we have to rule… You think we'll have time?"

Hrafn just shrugged. "Of course we'll have time! We are two to rule, so we'll act faster!"

Olaf's face eased into a blissful smile. "Good!" he drawled. Obviously, he was already looking forward to it.

"One more thing," Hrafn lifted his finger, his expression serious again. "We must keep an eye on mother. Last time she was very upset about the prophecy. We have to make sure it never happens again."

Olaf nodded seriously. "Yes! So, the flying snake…"

The big black raven croaked and spread its powerful wings. Strong and proud, it took off and rose to the clear blue sky. Carried by the fresh wind, it made a large circle above the ship, savoring the freedom and the lightness of the flight that birds are the only ones to know.

Author's Note

I guess, for every writer, names have a very special value. I believe that the name is a part of the personality: it determines people's character, behavior and sometimes even destiny.

To make it clear to everyone and to avoid any possible pronunciation confusion, I decided to enclose a name index.

Name index

Torgeir—[TOR-geyr]—"Thor's spear" (Old Norse).
Ari—[AH-ree]—"eagle" (Old Norse).
Orm—"snake" (Old Norse).
Advar—[ahd-VAHR]—"reach guard" (Old English).
Helgi—[HEH-lgee]—"blessed, holy" (Old Norse).
Halvdan—[HALF-dahn]—"half Dane" (Old Norse).
Gudmund—[GOOD-moond]—"god's protection" (Old Norse).
Turid—[TOO-ruhd]—"beautiful" (Old Norse).
Olaf—[OH-lahf]—"ancestor's descendant" (Old Norse).
Hrafn—"raven" (Old Norse). According to different sources, it can be pronounced as [RAPN] or [RAFN]. I prefer the second.

Harald—[HAH-rahlt]—"leader of the army" (Old Norse and Old English).

Örjan—[OE-rjan]—"farmer, earth worker" (Ancient Greek).

Ottar—[OH-tar]—"wealthy" (Old Germanic).

Kirk—"church" (Ancient Greek).

Sveinn—[SVEN]—"boy" (Old Norse).

Siv—"bride" (Old Norse). Siv was the wife of Thor in Norse mythology.

Eydis—[EY-dees]—"goddess of good fortune" (Old Norse).

Asta—[AH-stah]—"goddess of beauty" (Old Norse).

Knut—[KNOOT]—"knot" (Old Norse).

Idunn—[ee-DOON]—"love again" (Old Norse). Iðunn was the goddess of immortality and spring. She was responsible for guarding of the gods' apples of youth.

Ulfrich—[OOLF-reek]—"wolf's rule" (Old Germanic).

Jari—[YAH-ree]—a short form of Hjálmarr "helmeted warrior" (Old Norse).

Leif—[LAYF]—"descendant, heir" (Old Norse).

Vali—[VA-li]—"foreigner" (Old Norse).

About the Author

Dear reader,

First of all, thank you for picking up my book and for reading it. This book is my beloved creation. It represents ideas, characters and beliefs that are dear to me, which is why I feel both nervous and excited to share it with you.

Your remarks, questions and reviews are very welcome. When readers like you share their thoughts about my books on Amazon or any other place online it means a lot to me ;-) It does not have to be long and fancy, even a small paragraph is great.

Thank you! ;-)

Now, a quick word about myself.

I am an avid book reader. My number one preference is fiction, and even though I have a lot of favorite books and authors, Harry Potter still holds the top position ;-) I also appreciate some non-fiction books, especially related to psychology and communication. (Needless to say that a bookshop is the place where I can get lost to the world for hours) ;-)

Apart from that, I work as a conference interpreter. I love this job, because it allows me to discover a lot of interesting things about a wide variety of topics. And, most importantly, it makes me travel a lot.

As for my hobbies, I am an Irish dancer. I also love music and sometimes I write songs. If you are curious about those, go to my website http://www.ravenboy.com, and click on "Goodies".

By the way, extras and additional information related to the story is waiting for your there as well ;-)

Best wishes,

Kateryna Kei

The story continues in

BOOK 2

TWO PARTS OF A
SOUL

BY KATERYNA KEI

THE BABY

Within the depths of the forest, Old Nim knelt in the middle of a clearing. Tall, untamed plants and flowers grew randomly around her, nearly obscuring her from view. This place was her garden, though it didn't look much like one. Old Nim didn't look like a gardener, for that matter. She was small and thin. Her hair was long and naturally golden, and her wrinkled face was lit by a warm inner light. Her smiling, sky-blue eyes were still beautiful, reflecting both calmness and a childish curiosity about the world. Kneeling there among the tall herbs, the woman looked like some sort of fairy or a fantastic illusion.

It was one of those sweet summer evenings when the air is filled with the aroma of flowering heather and the relaxing hum of bumblebees, the type where the sunset pours its honey over the grass and the trees, drawing their long shadows across the ground.

That particularly placid evening, Old Nim was gathering the herbs; her long, thin fingers ran along every plant, carefully studying each leaf and stem and sensing the smallest details, which no ordinary person would notice. She selected only what she needed, leaving no trace of her collection and remaining in harmony with nature.

Suddenly, her hand froze over the leaf she was about to touch. A barely perceptible trembling of the ground under her knees told her that someone was approaching. No sound was audible yet, but years of experience had made her absolutely unparalleled in reading nature. She remained motionless for a while, her eyes closed, as if taking a quick reprieve, and then she calmly resumed her work.

Meanwhile, the noise sounded, first as a distant humming and then as a clear, alarming clatter of hooves. A moment later, a foaming horse frantically halted at the edge of the forest, right before the clearing. The rider was a young woman. She dismounted and ran toward Old Nim. Her beautiful face was covered with dust, and her long dark hair fell loose on her shoulders, spilling over her ornate gown.

Reaching Old Nim, the woman hastily fell to her knees.

"Nim," she called, panting, "help me!"

For the first time, Nim turned to face her, and her sky-blue eyes widened with concern and surprise when she saw the woman's gown was torn and covered in blood.

"It's a nightmare!" sobbed the young woman. She covered her face with her left hand, her right arm holding tight to a bundle.

Old Nim stood up and gently hugged the woman, patting her shoulder. "There, there," she said quietly, "calm down, for emotions blur your mind ..."

The woman abided, yet it took her some time to fully regain her composure. Finally, she stopped sobbing and straightened her back.

Nim waited in silence, her azure eyes shining with compassion and patience.

The young woman drew a deep breath and spoke, her voice quiet and strangely distant, as if she was in some sort of trance. "Father died right after midnight. Po wants me to marry him and to rule with him. I refused—it would have made no difference anyway for me, or for my people. Po then organized the rebellion against me—" she stopped, and her vacant glance widened with horror. "So many people died! It was ... It was ... I never imagined they could be so cruel to their own brothers and neighbors!" She closed her eyes, and her free hand formed a fist, as if in overwhelming agony. She growled painfully, like a fatally wounded animal.

Nim didn't let her dwell on the pain. "And your husband?"

The question had the effect of a slap to the face: the young woman straightened and looked at Nim, her glance alive and full of strength and fury.

"Po's got him, I'm sure of it! I saw it in his eyes. Po will do more than just kill him. That evil man wants to separate us forever … Nim, I have to do something!"

In front of the raging cauldron of emotions that was this young woman, Old Nim remained serene and undisturbed. She had lived long enough to learn how to remain calm in any situation. Still, her voice was firm and serious. "How can I help you?"

The young woman had been expecting these words with such anticipation that when they finally came, she found it hard to gather her thoughts. She swallowed and held out her bundle to Nim.

"I managed to save Anna …" Carefully unfolding a sheet, she lovingly caressed the tiny face of a baby. "My daughter… the living proof of our love …" she murmured with pride and affection before raising her eyes to Nim again. "Nim, I want you to take care of her."

Nim didn't say a word, and her face showed no new emotion, so the young woman went on. "I know I'm asking a lot, but you are our only chance! What Ronen is facing is worse than death. I must try and save him." Tears filled her eyes and spilled again, falling on the baby's cheek. She hurriedly wiped her face with her sleeve, but the baby woke up and smiled.

The mother bent and kissed the baby's forehead. "Anna, I love you," she whispered. "And your father loves you. Very, very much." She kissed the baby again and then spoke to

Nim, never taking her eyes off her daughter. "Nim, you are the only person I trust enough to care for her. If I do not return, she will be safe with you. I want her to grow up pure and honest, like a true daughter of her family, like a true granddaughter of her glorious grandfather!"

Nim stared thoughtfully into the young woman's face for a while. After several pensive moments, she slowly nodded and held her arms to the baby.

"I've never had a child of my own and am honored by your trust. Melaina, I promise you, I will do any and all things necessary to protect her."

The young woman tried to smile, her lips trembling with emotion. Blinking rapidly to chase away the tears, she mournfully stated, "Thank you, Nim. I will never forget it."

They remained silent for some time as both looked intently at the baby, who was watching them with interest. Melaina bent down to kiss her daughter for the last time and carefully gave the baby to Nim. Wiping away her tears, she stood up and hurried toward the horse, which was waiting right where she had left it.

When she got in her saddle, Nim called to her. "Melaina…"

She looked back.

"You are the best magician I ever knew. Stay calm, and listen to what your heart tells you. Gods help you!"

A sad smile washed over Melaina's face. She waved in a final goodbye, forever engraving in her memory the picture of the old woman kneeling in the middle of tall heather bushes and holding her only beloved daughter in her arms.

~~~
~~~

When Melaina was gone, Old Nim didn't linger. Quickly finishing her gathering, she put all the plants into a simple linen bag, then carefully hid all traces of human presence in the clearing. Her exit was as seamless and stealthy as her arrival.

Moving noiselessly and quickly for an old woman, she left no visible trace in her wake. The forest was her home, her element. She had been living there for ages, and no one was able to find or catch her there.

Soon she arrived at her hut, which was disguised with branches and plants. There she stopped to give the baby some fresh milk and to gather her most important possessions, which she fixed on her horse's back.

At nightfall, the small fellowship started their long journey east. It looked unusual and somewhat surreal: a small, fairylike woman, with her fair hair shining in the moonlight, a baby in her arms, and a horse and cow walking close behind her.

Nim was leaving. She didn't know whether she would ever come back, but she had given her word to Melaina. She was determined to protect the child by any means, even if she had to bear the pain of leaving home for the second time in her life.

THE COMEBACK

Anna grew up with Nim in the middle of a vast, dense forest. The fairy woman taught her how to talk to animals and plants, cast spells, make potions, and survive. At the same time, the girl had a truly royal education: she could sing, dance, play the flute, read, and write, and she learned good manners as well as the hierarchy of her people's society.

She looked more and more like her mother every day, with the exception of the color of her eyes: sky-blue, like her father's.

Nim taught her about the world through stories and tales, and she told her all that she knew about her parents.

When Anna was ten, Nim decided that it was time for them to go back, to try to find out what had happened after they left, as well as to have a glimpse of the present situation.

The girl was happy to travel and asked a lot of questions along the way.

"Aren't you tired of talking?" sighed Nim in a parental tone.

Anna rolled her eyes. "How can one get tired of talking? It takes so little effort—you are only moving your mouth! Tell me more about the sea! What are the good spirits living there like?"

Nim kept answering for a while longer but then concluded by stating, "Now it's my turn to ask questions. Tell me, which plants are you going to gather at full moon?"

Anna moaned with disappointment but answered, "Mistletoe, wild rose, lily of the valley, sea buckthorn, melissa, three-part beggarticks, inula, bearberry, and ledum."

"Aye, and also thyme. Don't forget it."

Before Nim could say anything else, Anna asked, "If you are making potions at black-moon night, are they going to affect the soul?"

"Not necessarily."

"But you said black-moon nights are for dark magic!"

"Aye, but dark magic does not deal only with souls."

"But you said the worst thing that can ever be done to someone is touching their soul!"

"Aye. If you kill the body, the soul is still alive, while if you harm the soul, you harm that person's existence in the Universe."

"It means that the person will not be able to live another life?"

Nim sighed and was visibly annoyed by this point in time. "Possibly. I don't know. But not all dark magicians are that evil. And, most importantly, very few of them are powerful enough for such spells. It's a very advanced and dangerous magic, one with a lot of power behind it. You should be aware of it, but make sure you have no other solution before trying it."

Anna thought for a while and went on with new energy. "Is Po evil enough? Does he deal with souls?"

Nim didn't answer right away. She thoughtfully studied her small hands and frowned slightly. "I cannot tell for sure. I haven't seen Po for many years now. He may have acquired that secret knowledge, for he used to experiment with complex dark spells and rituals."

She looked up and met Anna's curious gaze. "This is another reason for us to be very careful and alert. I don't want you to be scared or to panic, but remember that the less attention you attract, the better it will be for us."

Anna nodded. She remained silent for some time, but

soon her questions resumed their merciless rate. "Can a soul be destroyed?"

"Aye, in theory. But as far as I know, no human has ever done it. Generally, dark magicians would simply try to gain control over a soul or to imprison it somehow."

"Can you do it to a living person?"

"When you take control over a soul, the person must be alive, otherwise it's useless. It allows you to make the person act according to your will, generally in the name of doing some terrible things. You can recognize the affected people by the very drastic change in their behavior and by looking into their eyes—their pupils are always dilated, for their soul remains in the dark."

"And if you imprison a soul?"

"To imprison a soul, you must kill the person and catch the soul at the moment it is leaving the body. Then you have to put it somewhere and to surround it with spells that will hold it there. But it is very hard to do because a soul is not a physical object."

"And is there a way to get free of it?"

"Hardly, if the dark magician knows what he or she is doing. But then again, I don't know for sure. It's another reason for you to remember your protective spells, young lady. Come on, recite …"

Anna heaved a sigh. "All right, you win again … First there is …"

~~~

By sunset, they had arrived at Nim's previous home. It stood there as before, only now branches and tall wild herbs hid it completely, as if the hut had grown into the tree, becoming an integral part of the plants themselves.
~~~

Nim and Anna dismounted and walked carefully toward the hut. They looked like sisters playing an exciting game: the same height, the same dresses, waist-length free-flowing hair, and a similar slender shape. But while Nim's hair was bright golden, Anna's was black, and Nim's thin face was covered with lines, a reminder of the several hundreds of years that she had lived on Earth. Anna examined the place with obvious excitement and admiration, while Nim looked alert and tense, like a wild animal coming to the river.

They silently approached the hut from behind and made their way into the stable, where there was a hidden door leading into the hut. Anna didn't notice it, so when Nim suddenly pulled it open, she gasped in amazement.

Nim ordered the girl to remain in the stable then she carefully stepped into the hut and started examining it. She had an outstanding memory and knew exactly where she had left everything.

To her surprise, it looked like no one had been there after her sudden departure. There was no trace of Melaina, or of any other intruder. Prudent as she was, Nim checked the hut for any spells or traces of magic, just in case, but it was clean.

"May I come in?" Anna begged impatiently.

"You may now," Nim allowed, and the girl hurried inside.

The hut was very simple. It had two small windows, now completely hidden by wild plants, and just one room that served as kitchen, dorm, and living room all at the same time. There was a small fireplace and minimal furniture. The place was covered with layers of dust, but Anna loved it instantly.

"Where can I make myself a bed?" she asked, her voice eager.

Nim, who was busy smelling the potions that had remained there during all those years, looked at her with studied irritation. "Don't you think we ought to clean the place first?"

Anna shrugged innocently. "I wasn't intending to go to bed right now …"

~~~

The next morning, Nim took Anna to the sea, which she had never seen before. When they got to the rocky coast, Anna froze, speechless. Blue waves rolled toward the land from the very edge of the horizon to hit the rocks and fall down as white foam. Seagulls flew over the sparkling water, and their screams echoed around them. Anna took a deep breath, filling her lungs with salty air.

"Come, there is a beach down there," called Nim. "We'll swim."

Together, Nim and Anna swam and played in the water until Anna's lips turned blue with cold. Afterward, they lay on the sand, sunbathing. Nim showed Anna some edible mollusks and algae and explained how to eat them.

In the afternoon, they went to the clearing where Nim had last seen Anna's mother. The clearing looked just as it had before—randomly growing tufts of heather, their sweet-smelling pink flowers attracting insects and bumblebees.

Anna walked the path over and over, trying to imagine her mother doing it, trying to feel her thoughts and emotions at that moment.

"Do you have any idea what could have happened to them?" she asked finally.

Nim gave her a quick glance from behind a bunch of flowers that she was gathering. "Well, that's what I'm intending to find out here. There is no doubt—Melaina never came back here, or to my hut, after that day."
~~~

Anna's eyes sparkled with hope. "What can I do to help you?"

Nim didn't answer straight away. She carefully lowered her flowers on the grass then stood up and walked toward the girl. She put her hands on Anna's shoulders and met her gaze. "Anna, I'm sorry," she said quietly. "None of them are alive. I do not pretend to be the best magician, but I can surely feel when people dear to me die, and I felt Melaina dying. I don't know exactly what happened that day, or whether or not she was able to save your father. All I know is that she died willingly, and it may be important for us to know why."

Tears filled Anna's eyes. "Why didn't I feel that?"

"You certainly felt it! You started crying, and I was unable to calm you for quite a while. But you were too small to remember it."

The girl swallowed and looked away. "Do you think I need to become the queen?" she asked after a while.

"I wouldn't advise you to undertake that. At least not yet."

THE MEETING

Once a week, the town celebrated market day. Foreigners, travelers, and all sorts of traders arrived from a myriad of directions at dawn, and throughout the whole day, they sold or traded their goods in the streets of the town. This day was considered a holiday; it was a good opportunity for towns-folk to wear new clothes, to meet new people, and to simply entertain themselves.

That May morning, the sky was cloudless and blue, birds sang happily, and the gentle breeze carried the intoxicating smell of flourishing trees. Warm weather reanimated the trade, and the market was even more crowded than usual.

The most prestigious and expensive merchant rows were hidden from the sun under a removable roof made of tied pine tree branches. That place was the most crowded of all the rows, with acrobats, illusionists, and even gapers.

A tall bald man walked among the colorful crowd. He wore a long white silk tunic and matching cloak with golden embroidery. Several rings with differently shaped precious stones shone on his long fingers, and one large golden ring with engraved symbols circled his bald head. His face was pale and perfectly shaven, and he exuded a strong sense of power. His thin face, with an aquiline nose and beautifully shaped violet eyes, could have been considered handsome if not for his constant scowling expression and pursed lips. It was Po, the main priest and real ruler of the country.

That day, Po was in his usual bad mood, which his servants had come to consider the norm. The kingdom was gradually falling into a crisis, even though Queen Elena was completely under his control, yet it had nothing to do with his bad temper. The kingdom and its situation did not bother him much at all. Po made sure he would survive and keep all his wealth, no matter what. The people around him were too common and primitive to serve for anything but his magical experiments. All of them had weaknesses, and Po was so good at finding and using these weaknesses, that he was beginning to find it all becoming boring.

People feared the main priest. Po was well known for his cruelty and constant bad mood, but no one talked about it out of fear. Everyone knew that Po was a very skilled magician. Apart from him and his priests, no one was allowed to perform magic of any kind. All the magicians had been killed or banished from the town, and the use of magic of any kind was officially prohibited.

However, magic was the only thing that still interested Po, and he eagerly and greedily gathered secret knowledge from everywhere. Thus, he was coming to the market to keep an eye on people and at the same time to see whether foreign traders had something interesting for use in his magical studies.

Two guards and a slave boy accompanied him. Not that Po really needed guards; his magical knowledge was more than sufficient to protect him from any possible attack. He was only using them to intimidate the townspeople as well as to show his importance and high social stature. On the other hand, the guards were useful when the main priest had to do something dirty publicly, like punishing some scum.

Po's slave boy was small, disproportionate, and even somewhat girlish. He was obviously from the north, for his skin was pale and his hair was very blond. He was seven, but ill fed and bony as he was, he looked younger. There was something animalistic in his furtive, lurking glance and in his bent shoulders. He looked as if he was always expecting a kick. The boy was barefoot, and his rough oversized tunic made his bony body, with its long arms and legs, look grotesque. Moreover, his colorless eyes shone with hate, only increasing the unpleasant impression he was producing.

Po held his slave on a large silver chain, which ended with a ring that was constantly locked around the boy's neck. When he was angry, or just wanted to punish the boy, he pulled on the chain, causing his victim immense suffering.

The guards escorting Po were total opposites of the slave boy, very tall and muscled. Taller and wider than the main priest himself, they were obviously well fed and cared for, and they appeared to be relaxed, looking around with lazy indifference. They knew that their appearance alone, with menacing swords on the hip and glittering metallic armbands around their colossal forearms, dissuaded any attempt to get closer to the procession.

Po walked slowly among the foreign traders. Organization was definitely missing within the market: nuts, spices, and fruits were sold right next to furs, jewels, stones, and dishes. Po deeply disapproved of it, but he knew from experience that it was the best place to purchase interesting things. There were even a couple of traders from whom he consistently bought items.

One of them, a small, fat man with a ponytail and quick, cunning eyes, spotted the priest from afar. A greedy sparkle lit his small eyes and made his lips part in a cheesy smile. All the traders knew that Po was a real moneybag, and if there was something, even a useless little thing that caught his attention, the price never bothered him.

Po stopped in front of the fat man and coldly answered his greetings.

"Do you still have that crystal cup you brought last time?" asked the priest.

The trader's heart sank. "Your Highness, unfortunately, someone bought it from me last month." He was genuinely sorry to have to disappoint his best customer. "But I've got something special to show you—"

"Who bought it?" Po cut him short, without paying even a speck of attention to his sales pitch.

The man's eyes rolled as he tried to recall the details. "It was a lady traveler. She was moving east with her new husband and wanted the cup for her jewels," he answered finally.

Po nodded. No emotion showed on his face, but he felt satisfied.

Taking it as a good sign anyway, the trader resumed his strategy. "I want to show you something, Your Highness ..." he started conspiringly. "I got my hands on it by pure chance and thought of you just as I saw it ..." He hurriedly dived under his counter and started searching his boxes.

"Of course, you don't have to buy it," Po heard his muffled voice. "But as this object is unique and extremely rare, I think you should see it."

He emerged from under the counter red-faced and panting, he was simply not in good enough shape for such endeavors. His eyes shone, and his fat, short-fingered hand held a small leather parcel. Carefully unfolding the parcel, he displayed its contents to the priest.

Po remained impassive, yet even before he saw the item that was inside, he knew he had to have it. What he saw surpassed his wildest expectations: he was holding a palm-sized, perfectly round blood-red ruby. Just as the daylight touched it, the ruby started shining with a mysterious red light. The stone looked alive, as if it had its own powerful and capricious personality. It seemed as if it was observing the people around it, reading their deepest thoughts and fears.

Po watched the ruby, speechless. He was more than fascinated.

"It is called the 'Dragon's Eye,'" the trader whispered mysteriously. "It's a unique gem from a big island far in the south. People say it has a very strong character and can even kill …"

While Po was admiring the red stone, his guards grew bored, waiting for their master. Yawning lazily, they looked around at the women passing by. The slave boy, taking advantage of everybody's lack of attention, slowly started moving toward the neighboring counter, where a couple of noisy women were buying fruits. Big and juicy white peaches were lying there and calling to him. The boy had never tasted one before, but the sweet smell emanating from them was so appealing, and his stomach had been empty since the previous morning. Unable to resist the temptation, he decided to steal one of those beautiful fruits, or at least to die trying, for his life was tough and worthless anyway.

Trying to look casual and to not attract attention, he slowly moved toward the peaches, which formed a tidy pyramid at the edge of the counter. Blankly staring at the ground, he felt more aware of the world around him than ever, observing the people around him with every cell of his body.

It seemed to him that a lot of time passed until he finally got to the wooden counter where the fruits were laid. There, he dared lift up his head and looked around.

The two women were arguing loudly with the trader about the price, and Po and his guards were not watching.

Moving very smoothly, he reached out and seized the closest peach.

Again, no one seemed to notice.

A wave of pleasurable anticipation swept over him.

As he pulled the fruit toward him, however, the whole pyramid moved slightly.

Petrified, the child froze. The thought of what would happen to him if the whole pile fell down sent a cold shiver down his spine. Irritated by the sweet smell, his stomach started rumbling even louder, and the desire to taste the beautiful fruit became so overwhelming that, shaking with fear, he held out his free hand and grabbed an orange from the bag of one of the arguing women. Then, quickly removing the peach, he stuffed the orange in its place.

The peach pyramid shivered slightly but did not fall.

Sneaking the stolen peach under his tunic, the boy slowly moved back. Struggling to keep his knees from shaking, he hid himself behind Po. Only then did he finally dare to breathe.

Meanwhile, the fat trader was triumphantly closing the sale; Po was obviously very interested. His eyes were fixed on the stone, and his nostrils flared nervously. He bent forward toward the trader, catching every single word.

"See, there is a round emptiness right in the middle of the stone. An air bubble, I guess. Its color is always slightly different. It makes the stone look like a living eye that watches you. This species is absolutely unique, and it needs a master whose power can overpower its own, otherwise—"

"How much?" interrupted Po, his voice calm and firm again.

"Fifteen metretes of gold," answered the trader, and instantly regretted it. It was nearly ten times the price he had paid for the stone, and it was too much, even for a man as rich as the main priest.

The latter slowly looked at the trader. His pupils were narrow, and it was impossible to read anything in his cold violet stare. He stared unblinkingly at the trader for several eternal heartbeats, and the fat man's anxiety skyrocketed. He cursed his consuming greed, nearly sure that he had just lost his best client.

Suddenly, the priest spoke.

"I'll give you two metretes right now, and I'll keep the stone. As for the rest of the gold, my servants will bring it to you by sunset."

The trader's heart leaped happily in his chest. He had trouble suppressing a huge sigh of relief. He rubbed his hands together, discovering that they were sweaty, which was appropriate, considering how frightened he had been.

"Deal, Your Highness. Anyway, I was not intending to leave before tomorrow."

Po wasn't really listening. Carefully covering the stone with leather, he hid the parcel safely in his pocket and was intending to pay as agreed, when a shriek made him jump.

"You, you little thief!"

Po swiveled on his heels and quickly assessed the situation. It was a woman who had shrieked, and the trader from the closest counter was now yelling with her, angrily pointing in Po's direction.

"He stole my fruit!"

Fruits were the very last thing Po was interested in, so he instantly understood what might have happened. Without even looking back, he jerked the silver chain fixed around his forearm.

Petrified by the screams and panic, and blinded by a sudden and violent pain, the slave boy fell on the ground, coughing and fighting for air. The half-eaten peach fell from his juice-covered hand and rolled in the dust.

Po slowly turned around to watch the boy suffering. He pulled violently on the chain again and again.

Wheezing and wriggling in the dust, his helpless victim

was in agony, nearly asphyxiated. The boy's face went red. The metallic ring cut deep into his skin, and fresh blood ran on the collar of his tunic. Tears ran down his face, dust filled his mouth and nostrils.

The guards watched the boy's agony in amusement, leaning lazily against the large wooden columns that supported the roof.

The crowd of onlookers formed a circle around the priest and his prey, some of them petrified, while others became excited at the sight of blood and suffering.

The main priest kept pulling on the chain, again and again. His violet eyes shone with immense satisfaction in his cold, stone-like face. Absolutely deaf to the child's pain, he seemed unable to get enough of the mere sight of suffering.

"Stop it!"

A small figure suddenly jumped out of the crowd and seized the silver chain.

The crowd gasped at the daring of this skinny, dark-haired girl. Po froze, taken by surprise.

Quick as a flash, the girl knelt by the slave and touched the ring at his neck. Maybe the lock couldn't stand the repeated harsh pulling, or maybe there was some other reason entirely, but the ring sprang open, releasing the boy.

Still coughing and swallowing for air, the slave clung to her arm as if it was a source of life, receiving the healing energy she was sending him.

Meanwhile, Po was back to his senses. He was given a new, fresh victim to punish! His thin lips twisted in anticipation of the new pain. Slowly savoring the moment, he raised his free arm, ready to cast a spell upon the girl.

As if she felt his intention, the girl looked up at him, and their eyes met.

The priest's eyes widened. He suddenly felt breathless. All

the blood left his face, and he instantly forgot the spell he was about to use.

It could not be true. It was unbelievable! It was her! Hers was the face that had been haunting him for so many years! A flow of memories washed over Po, fresh and painful, as if it had happened only yesterday. A beautiful young witch with unknown ancient magic. She had to belong to him! He had been plotting everything for years, through suffering and humiliation, and he had been so close to his aim, so close! But she left him with the bitter, consuming anger of defeat and with burning, unsatisfied desires. She was the source of his dearest aspirations and deepest pain. He thought he would never see her again, but miraculously, here she was!

The girl wasn't disturbed by his reaction. Awarding the priest a disdainful glance, she said angrily, "Shame on you! He's just a boy! It's so easy to hurt someone too weak to fight back!"

She looked down at the boy, who was still panting, his head now lying on her knee.

Po remained silent. He needed to calm down. He took a deep breath to slow down his madly racing heart. "Would you prefer me to hurt someone stronger?"

The girl blinked in disbelief. "I don't want you to hurt anyone at all!"

Po couldn't take his eyes off her. He still couldn't believe it was not an illusion. He would keep her. She belonged to him. It was logical. She was his reward for so many years of suffering. Struggling to regain control over his swirling thoughts, he asked, "What's your name?"

The girl flashed him a dirty look, intending to respond, but Po never heard what she said. With a deafening crack, a wooden column supporting the roof broke under the back of one of the guards.

The man yelled with pain and fear, falling backward.

The crowd shrieked, drowning all the other noises.

Instinctively, the guard tried to stop himself, seizing the edge of the fruit counter, and it crashed too, covering the man with a hopping and rolling avalanche of fruits and vegetables.

For some time, panic seized the crowd. Screaming in fear, people moved chaotically away from the crash. However, the roof didn't fall completely; only one of its edges hung low above the stands. Little by little, the panic stopped.

Standing among the dusty fruits, Po stared at the broken chain on the ground. Both the girl and the slave were gone. Anger and disappointment washed over him, making him snarl like a wounded animal. "Where is she?" he yelled at the other guard. The latter could only shrug helplessly.

"Find her!" he barked as he threw the chain on the ground. He did not need it any longer.

"Watch me, Melaina," he muttered to himself. "Who will win now that you're back?"…

Milton Keynes UK
Ingram Content Group UK Ltd.
UKHW040615210324
439796UK00001B/83